ABBIE

COLLISION OF MINDS

Annita Clarke

Published by New Generation Publishing in 2020

First Edition

ISBN
       Paperback   978-1-80031-932-5
       Hardback   978-1-80031-931-8

www.newgeneration-publishing.com

New Generation Publishing

Dedication

I would like to dedicate this, my first book and a lifelong ambition, to my husband Steve, who has always supported me and to our fantastic, wonderful children Olivia and Matthew.

CHAPTER 1

The Painful Disclosure

Newspaper article. Luton News 11 January 2019.

FATAL ROAD COLLISION CLOSES MOTORWAY AT RUSH HOUR

The Southbound M1 was closed from yesterday lunchtime as a result of a two-vehicle collision. During the collision, a Vauxhall Corsa driven by a man in his late teens, collided with a Seat Ibiza, travelling along the motorway towards Luton. The offending vehicle was driven down the slip road at speed onto the motorway at junction 11 and collided with the nearside front and rear of the Seat, spinning this vehicle into the central reservation, bringing the motorway to a halt. Ambulance, fire and police were called to the scene.

The two young passengers within the Seat received massive injuries. The front seat passenger, a boy of nine years received fatal injuries and died whilst still at the scene. The rear seat passenger, a girl of fourteen years, remains in Saint Matthews Hospital in an induced coma, as a result of her injuries. There are no updates in relation to her condition at this time. The driver of the Corsa, believed to live in the area, received superficial injuries and was released from Saint Matthews Hospital last night.

The motorway remained closed for police investigation throughout the night and diversions are still in place. Police have stated that they are investigating the incident from a criminal perspective and will be interviewing the driver of the Corsa in due course.

Anyone with any dashcam footage or any information in relation to the collision is invited to contact Sgt John Munroe, Collision Investigation Unit (CIU), Bedfordshire, Cambridgeshire and Hertfordshire (BCH) Roads Policing Department, who is the officer in charge of this enquiry.

#

Abbie lay unconscious in her hospital bed. She was unaware of Jamie's death. Her annoying little brother. The boy who she taught to tie his shoelaces and build Lego cities, play hide and seek and use a knife and fork. He was no longer around, and she would not be able to share any more birthdays, Christmases or days out ever again. The bond between them was something that surpassed the normal brother and sister relationship. It's often said that when considering twins, they understand each other and often feel pain when the other is injured, and may feel sad or happy depending on how the twin is feeling at the time, irrespective of the city or country they are in or the distance between them. Weirdly, this is how Abbie had felt about Jamie. There had always been that relationship, that unexplained connection, but she would no longer have him with her.

Numerous physicians and doctors continually surrounded her bed checking all monitors numerous x-rays, CT scans and blood work, whispering short, hushed sentences. The looks between them were undistinguishable and their meanings could not be determined by anyone witnessing these transactions. Her coma had been induced as her brain had swelled immediately after the incident due to the massive impact on her left side.

#

Alison had been driving the vehicle at the time of the incident. She was now the mother of a deceased nine-year-old boy and an unconscious fourteen-year-old girl. Her life, her dreams and a future all changed in an instant. If Abbie was not still holding on to life by her fingertips, Alison knew she could not have continued. It was all too painful. She was having to deal with this alone as her husband James, who had been a police officer for ten years, had committed suicide three years earlier. He had ended his life and consequently, and less importantly, his career in cybercrime. In his suicide note he had described the helplessness of investigating the most heinous child-related crimes, compiling evidence and charge files for court, only to find that the new gap in the market was rapidly filled by another abuser, rendering more children to the horror he was trying so hard to prevent. Having lost her husband of fifteen years, Alison had made Abbie and Jamie her world. Things had been tough, financially and emotionally. There was some money that was given to her and the children via the benevolent fund from the police, which is provided to any surviving immediate family following a serving officer's death, but even when putting this, together with the widow's pension from the government and Alison's meagre salary from her managers job at the local supermarket, it meant that belts were definitely tight. Abbie, a tall, slim, popular girl had excelled in any sport she had attempted and was a sought-after player,

3

however, the family's lack of funds and the regular trips to the school charity shop for hand-me-down uniform had been a source of ridicule from some of the less than pleasant pupils in Abbie's year. Ordinarily, she would be able to shrug this off, but she was now getting to an age where image meant something, and she had begun to bite back. There had also been a few issues recently with attitude and behaviour at home, staying up late, spending way too long on social media and missing homework deadlines. Alison had attributed the reasons for this change in behaviour to the death of their father and the typical teenager angst. Prior to the collision, Alison was making some headway on rebuilding their relationship, but Abbie had refused grief counselling, and both had reached a brick wall. On the other hand, Jamie was devastated when his father passed away. He had been unable to move forward and cried during the night, most nights, gripping onto Roger, the teddy that he had received from his parents for his birthday prior to his father's death. He had become insular, where his natural character was happy and playful. Jamie had attended counselling willingly. It appeared to be helping him to come to terms with his father's death and there was some progress in his ability to control his mood. There were fewer extremes and his outbursts were less dramatic. In fact, they were on their way to Jamie's counselling session when the collision occurred, ironically.

Today, Alison found herself, as she usually did at nine o'clock in the morning, two hours before visiting time, sitting by the bedside of her daughter. The nurses had long since ignored the timings of her visits and as long as she sat out of the way of the nurses, doctors and consultants she could sit and watch her child sleep. The numerous cards, balloons and flowers that decorated the room in which Abbie slept were sent by local and national readers of newspapers and viewers of news and YouTube videos. Alison despaired at the horrific reality that the general public had been viewing video images of the scene of the accident, she found it completely heart-breaking. Their lives had been played on the silver screen and although the situation had been taken into the hearts and minds of just so many people, it felt to Alison that their tragedy had been a money-spinner for florists and card makers around the country. These objects of sympathy had been sent by people who really didn't know the magic of Abbie and Jamie.

#

Thankfully, Abbie woke up five days after the collision. The consultants had chosen to manage this awakening slowly as there had been worrying signs on the various CT scans indicating a continuing swelling around her brain. This dangerous transition from comatose to awake was thoroughly managed and meticulously monitored.

As drugs were reduced and invasive intervention was slowly removed, it was some relief to her mother that she could finally see her child flicker her eyes, although Abbie was not receptive, she was now showing signs of life.

In the hospital room there continued to be the whirring and beeping from the remaining machines that were hooked up to Abbie. This non-ceasing rhythm gave a mixture of hope and despair as the need for this intervention was frightening but the lack of need due to a graver prognosis would have been worse.

Abbie came around very slowly. Still unaware of the devastating loss of her brother when she initially opened her eyes.

#

As I wake, I can feel that my legs and arms are laying on a crisp, cold surface. I can hear the loud melodious beeping of something on my right. Everything aches. There is a banging in my head, a pulse which seems to grip from the inside-out. Where am I and what has happened? I start to open my eyes, very slowly. There is so much light, it is blinding, white walls, a huge window to my left, where I am facing. It is daytime, although what time it is, I have not got a scooby. From the sounds and the clinical smells, I guess I am in hospital. From miles away, it sounds, I hear Jamie say, "Come on, Abbie, wake up lazybones…" This makes me smile.

"Oh my God!" I hear from my right. "Nurse, nurse, come quickly, she's awake!" My mum, oh my God, how long have I been asleep, if waking up is such big news? I try to look at her, but my head is killing me, preventing me from turning my head in her direction, and I hear myself groan. The whole of my left leg is agony, but it seems to come from my foot. What happened to it, why is it so sore?

"Oh no, sweetheart … lay still," My mum grabs my hand, "Abbie, Abbie you're going to be okay, it's going to be okay." I hear several people bustling into the room, I can't see them as the door is on my right.

A nurse leans over me and pulls my eye lid up, opening my left eye fully. It is excruciating. The light is far too bright. It's like when my best friend Sky got off the plane in Florida and the sunlight hit her on the steps to the runway. Her sunglasses weren't strong enough to cope with the brightness. It's the same now. I try to bury the back of my head into the cushion I'm leaning on. "When did she wake up?" the nurse asks my mum. She's abrupt but I guess they need to get the facts, but she makes it sound so urgent. I am really worried now.

"Just now, she just smiled and started open her eyes. Is she okay? Will she be okay?"

A female doctor comes around to my left and I can see her face. She looks kind and cups the left side of my face with the palm of her right hand. Her hand is soft and warm. She looks past me, probably to my mum and says, "We will have to take things slowly, but the signs are good." She looks down to me and seems to examine my face closely. I would normally be uncomfortable with this sort of attention, but it feels completely natural. Maybe it's her white coat that gives me the feeling of reassurance? Either way, I feel safe. Wait a minute, I feel safe but where is Jamie? I heard him but I can't see him. He probably left or is under the bed.

#

"Are you hungry, sweetheart?" my mum asks me. I feel hungry but I'm not sure if I am going to be able to keep anything down.

"Let me get you something, there was a tuna sandwich at the café, nice and soft. You like tuna, don't you?" Mum stands up. She had moved her chair around

7

to the left side of my bed so that I didn't have to move to see her. I saw her lean down, as she stands, her large black shopping bag is in her hands.

"Mum," I say, my throat is so sore, I sound croaky, not like me. I can see that she looks scared. Is it about what I may say, what I might ask? "I won't be a minute, sweetheart. Will you be okay?" she holds my wrist, narrowly missing the canular in the back of my hand. She doesn't hold my gaze, but I can see she has been crying.

As she leaves the room, I hear the door close gently. I don't watch her leave as turning my head is still too painful. I look out of the window, squinting at first, until I can bear the light. I can see the tops of the hospital building, the flat rooves and various grills and chimneys. Beyond the red brick of the vast building and the spacious, albeit, full car park, is the motorway. The thickness of the glass prevents the vehicle sounds from interrupting the heart monitors and other machines beeping on the right side of my bed. As the light starts to fade (or maybe I am just getting more used to the brightness of the day), I can see the cars and lorries travelling on both sides of the six carriageways, half going one way, half, the other. I wonder about the lives of those in the cars, what they are talking about, what they are listening to on the radio and where they are going. A bird flies past my window, a pigeon, I think. Rats with wings, my granddad used to call them. I remember Jamie chasing them on Trafalgar Square in London, near Nelson's Column, I think. God, everything is so hazy. A mixture of thoughts, all flooding in at once.

I manage to slowly ease my head round to the right. The pain is intense around the back of my head and down the right side of my neck and shoulder. I can't manage all the way around, but even part of the way around allows me to see the door and the people entering and leaving. It was only a few minutes later that my mum bustles back into the room. Struggling with two packs of canteen sandwiches and two cups of tea in plastic cups, she awkwardly opened the door to my isolated room with her elbow pushing the door open with the back of her hand carrying the sandwiches. "I got you tuna on rye; I know how you like it. I checked the packet, no nuts" she said. I look at the sandwich and internally gag. Not my usual choice of breakfast, considering it seems that I have just woken up from the longest sleep I had ever had.

"Thanks, Mum," I struggle to open the cellophane of the sandwich, there appears to be little strength in my hands, manipulating vacuum packed sandwiches beats me at the best of times, but now it's nigh on impossible. Mum smiles as she relieves me from this difficult task, opening the packet and handing me half a sandwich. I take a bite from the corner. "It's nice," I tell her, with a mouth full. I notice that she looks pleased but there is something behind her eyes. Something is wrong.

I am still eating my second half of my sandwich when the nurse walks in. "How are you feeling, dear? Are you warm enough? How's the pain?" Even if I could comprehend the questions, they appear to be rhetorical, as she doesn't provide space for a response or appear concerned that she may have missed the reply. She is about fifty years old, pragmatic, with a calming voice and has clearly worn her uniform through several years as it must have fitted her when she collected it, although it is struggling now. She has a pleasant face but the number of patients she must tend to have made her appear slightly uncaring or efficient (depending on your perspective). She takes my left hand and feels at the wrist for my pulse, looking down at the watch pinned upside down on her copious chest. She then takes my blood pressure, allowing the machine to tighten and then slacken around my arm. The machine peeps and she notes the required stats on the graph. "Doing well," she says. She replaces the clipboard at the bottom of the bed and walks out of the room.

I look at Mum. She looks older somehow. It's only been a few days, I think. In fact, I don't know exactly what happened or why I am here. It is something serious, I don't know enough people to justify the number of flowers and cards around the room. I don't know where Jamie is and why he hasn't come in to see me. I heard him at one point but haven't seen him at all. It's not like there is a Hazchem risk with me, Mum comes in, so, where is he?

#

"Mum, where's Jamie?" I ask. I look at her and she doesn't look at my face. Her hands are gripped in her lap. "Mum, what's going on?"

"Oh sweetheart," she says. She looks up and is crying. Large, wet tears rolling down both cheeks. She moves her chair closer to the bed. To be closer to me or to steady herself?

"Mum?" I am feeling really scared now.

"There was nothing anyone could do," she sobs. "Oh my God, they tried so hard to get him out of the car, but his injuries, they were… it was terrible." She looked around for someone to hold her hand. It was times like this that she needed my dad, when he should be here. No one should have to have this type of conversation, certainly not alone. "I am so sorry, sweetheart, but Jamie died in the accident. He's gone, Abbie… I am so sorry." She is crying properly now, and she leans forward, for comfort, or to support me, or both, I'm not sure.

I hug her back; I am scared but confused. "Jamie can't be dead, I heard him. He spoke to me." I shake my head. "There has been a mistake." I pull my hand away from her. I won't accept this, it's not real.

CHAPTER 2

Everything Is Going to Be Different

"Abbie, sweetheart, what do you mean that you heard him?" she asks. Her voice is a little calmer, but it does sound a little patronising.

It makes me cross, I'm not ten years old, I didn't imagine it. "It was when I was coming around, I heard him. I can't remember exactly what he said but he encouraged me to wake up, called me 'lazybones'." I look at her with pleading eyes, this has been the only indication that I had that he was still alive, and I was desperate to hold on to it.

"You were under heavy sedation; it was your mind playing tricks on you. Like a dream. Bless you, darling, he wasn't there. He died in the car." She leaned forward and gripped my arm. I shook her off.

"No, I DID hear him. Get out!" What she was saying was ridiculous. Jamie could not be gone. He was always so full of life. A ball of energy. I need him.

Both of us were crying. My mum's face was obscured by the handkerchief she had been wiping her eyes with. She blew her nose quietly and looked up towards me, her eyes red and bloodshot. "Please Abbie, we need to be strong for each other, we are all we have now. I love you so much."

"He can't be dead, Mum." I said, "we can't lose him too." I am sobbing. My thoughts immediately flashed to the terrible day three years ago when Mum had sat me down to tell me about dad. About how he had taken too many of the anti-depressants he had been prescribed and had been found in the garage of our house hanging. We knew that he was depressed and that he was slowly changing, becoming someone different, but at eleven, how could I possibly know the extent of his anguish or what I could really do to help, to stop this from happening? It was Mum that found him. She was returning home from work and about to start the dinner prep for mine and Jamie's return from school, when she saw his car at home. This was unusual as he was normally at work into the late hours, so she searched the house, looking for him. Unsuccessful, she went into the garage where he often would sit and read his motorbike magazines. He didn't own a motorbike now but had previously told us about the bikes he had owned and ridden in the past. He would recite long stories, describing the journeys he had been on and accidents he had both witnessed and been involved in. He always said that it was when he became a dad that he wouldn't risk his life for the sake of a bike ride. It was when Mum had entered the garage that she found him with a small stool turned over, near his feet.

It was the finality of the situation that affected Mum so much, I guess. We had all knew he was struggling, but we ploughed ahead hoping that he was going to find something that helped him, the medication, counselling or the self-help guides, something to make what he was feeling bearable. He couldn't talk to us about the horrific stuff he was seeing at work, the long, torturous hours or the people he was trying to look after, but it was affecting him and that was obvious. He still loved us, I'm sure, but he rarely spent time with us, and I couldn't remember the last time that I saw him smile. Mum was now a single parent to two children, but in truth, hadn't she really been that for some time? The whole situation had affected Jamie most of all. He needed his dad, but he wasn't there for him. So, Mum should have been, but she wasn't either. I guess that's when me and Jamie became so close. We had to be. Mum had become a vacuum, completely vacant and disappeared into 'just existing' but that's not enough. I resented her for this. I was only eleven and shouldn't have been expected to do what she should have been doing. Her voice brought me back to the dreadful reality of today.

"I am sorry, but he is gone. It was a terrible accident, so sudden."

"Mum, I need to know what happened, tell me. No one talked to us when dad passed, everyone told us we were too young. Well, if we are **it** now, we need to be honest with each other. I need to know. I'm not a kid anymore, Mum." Pleading with her, I squeezed her arm. She looked at me and nodded weakly.

She started quietly, I guessed she was testing my emotions at first, to see if I could deal with the detail. "The other car came from nowhere. So fast, I didn't see him. I couldn't do anything to stop it. When the car hit us, it threw our car over the other lanes and into the central reservation. The noise was deafening, metal against metal. The wheels spinning and skidding on the tarmac. Screaming in the car." She looked white; her eyes kept closing. She was pinching them shut, almost as if the reciting of the scene created the relived image in her mind and she was trying to shut it out

"Then everything stopped. The car was filled with dust and debris. Jamie's toys were strewn around the car and as I looked at both of you. There was so much blood. The airbags had gone off. I struggled to see past them and some of the dust got into my eyes. God, it stung.

The car was destroyed on your side and the whole of that side of the car had crumpled inwards, trapping you and Jamie. It was awful. I will never forget your screams, and the absolute silence from Jamie." Her sobs were louder now. She was gripping my arm desperate for the strength to complete the picture.

"I tried so hard to get out of the car, but my door was stuck against the barrier that separated north from south-bound traffic. I could not get out, I tried so hard but couldn't get away from what I knew... I could see that the accident had hurt Jamie seriously and he wasn't moving but I couldn't get out, I couldn't help him." She looked spent. Exhausted. Her tears had continued to fall but it appeared like a weight had been lifted slightly. Is this the first time that she had talked through the accident? Surely the police had wanted to talk to her, or maybe it was the conversation with me that she had been dreading and now, like an artist fears the first stroke of paint on the white canvas, she had opened that door and begun the worst conversation a parent could have with their child. She was now silent. Her explanation had been manic, like she needed to say everything before she lost her nerve, but with it all said she looks deflated. I am struggling to take it in. It answers why I am in this state in the hospital, why I have obviously been here for so long and why the well-wishers have felt compelled to share my grief, the grief that even I didn't know I was going to feel.

"What about the driver?" I asked. "The driver of the other vehicle, the one that hit us?"

"A short time after everything had stopped and our car had spun into the central reservation, I saw a young man come to the car. He was probably about mid-twenties, dark hair. He looked scared to death."

"Mum, don't feel sorry for him, he killed Jamie, he could have killed all of us." What did I just say? He killed Jamie, oh my God, killed Jamie, does that mean that I believe it? Why would my mum lie about that? Although, if he did kill Jamie, he should pay! There are no excuses, how could there be? I was incensed, shocked at her reaction. Benevolence is one thing, but this man is no more than a murderer. "When did the police arrive? Did they arrest him?"

"The police arrived a little while after the ambulance. They arrived first, then the fire engines and the police. There was chaos. I heard the police wanting to close the road, but I guess it's not that easy to close the M1 – the diversions must be hard to organise. Anyway, I saw the police speaking to the man I saw at the car. They took him to one of their cars and then I saw him being taken to an ambulance. The firemen moved our car off the central reservation, and I was able to get out of the car. The paramedics helped you out of the car, they put you on a stretcher, you had injured your left ankle during the accident, the side of the car had trapped your foot and Jamie's seat had moved backwards onto it. The paramedics wheeled you straight into an ambulance and I know that you were given a high dose of pain relief as you seemed to drift in and out of sleep at that point. They were worried about your neck and a brace was put on you. Whilst all this was going on, there were other firemen trying to pull the car frame from Jamie. A paramedic had struggled to find a pulse, there was one, but it was weak. I willed him to breathe. I couldn't get near him, there were too many people trying to get him out, keep him safe, treat him, keep him alive. I felt so helpless." She was breathing heavily now; her words were getting manic. Tears were flowing again, and she was holding her chest with the hand holding the handkerchief. "They managed to get him out of the car and took him straight to the floor. I walked around the people kneeling next to him and looked at him. He looked so, so pale. I saw them doing CPR, talking to him, 'Come on, Jamie'. I asked him to live, I kept on saying, we needed him, loved him and we couldn't live without him.

She continued, "One of the paramedics looked around at me, he looked so sad and he said, 'I'm sorry', shaking his head slowly. I collapsed to my knees. No one caught me, they were working on Jamie. I was crying, I screamed, 'No!' I couldn't believe it. He was so small, only a little boy. Such a good, kind little boy, my little boy. I had already lost your dad; I couldn't lose Jamie. It's not fair. Not on any of us."

I was crying now. She was right, he was too young to die. "Why did I survive? Why couldn't I have died, and he live? I don't want to be here; I want to be with Jamie and dad." I was hardly understandable; words were mumbled between sobs and I struggled to understand the loss. I had never felt so alone. Since dad died, Jamie had been my solace. We had helped each other to get through. We had hugged each other when we were sad and played well together whenever we could. His hide and seek was legendary, I can't believe there will be no more games, I wouldn't hear his laugh again saying, "Cold, warmer, hot, you found me!"

"I don't even remember the accident really, how can that be? I can't even remember the last thing I said to

Jamie, what he said to me." I feel completely lost, like half a person. "When was the accident?" I needed to get a reference, how long had I been here? How long since I saw him?

"The accident was a week ago, you have been in a coma for five days and they only brought you around properly today. I have been here every day, willing you to stay with me but dreading this conversation. I am so sorry, sweetheart." She looks drained, the stuffing has been knocked out of her. We are both still crying, but we are quieter now. Can't take it in fully.

"I am so sorry, sweetie, but we are going to have to talk about Jamie's funeral soon. I was going to start arranging it, but I thought you might want to help me. You were so close, and you know what he would want, his favourite music, the clothes he should wear, anything that he would like with him…" She looks pleadingly to me, I know that she needs to feel useful, but this feels too soon for me. Too final. "Have a think, we could make it all about him and his favourite things, really special."

"Can we do it a little later, Mum?" I ask. Unwittingly, I am already picturing him in his favourite jeans and jumper, the one with the Minecraft characters on it and his light and dark teddy bear, Roger, which was his final birthday present from dad. Panic struck me, "Roger, he was in the car with us, Jamie was holding him, I remember him putting him through the gap on his headrest, so he was looking at me in the back of the car. Is he still there?"

"No, sweetie. They brought him out. I have him. Do you think Jamie would like to have Roger with him?" I know Mum is cajoling me to try and occupy me and although I want to be stubborn and not join in with this morbid conversation, it helps somehow. "Yes, I think he would, he never went anywhere without him."

"That's settled then, Roger it is." She smiles a very weak smile, like one task has been ticked off a long and difficult list.

Dr Redmond enters the room. She is a tall, slim woman of around fifty years old. She has a northern, perhaps Mancunian accent and a kind nature. I remember her as the doctor whose hand had cupped my face as I awoke. There is an air of confidence about her and this is so reassuring. With everything else seemingly going wrong, she has the capability to make things right. Not true, of course, but it's something to hold on to.

"Well," she says, as she looks at the clipboard hooked over the bottom frame of my bed. "You gave us all quite a scare for a while, Abbie." She looks up and smiles at me, "but aside from a small patch of your head, the swelling has completely gone, and that area is smaller than yesterday, so we are definitely heading in the right direction." She looks at my mum, smiles and then looks at my left leg. Dr Redmond lifts the thin white blanket from my leg and exposes a plaster cast leg which had shiny steel rods poking out of both sides of the ankle and lower leg. My foot is cast to the toes and there are crumbs of plaster lying around the bottom of the sheet, obviously rubbed off the leg during my long sleep.

I'm shocked, I seem to remember my left leg hurting at the time but as I woke up, my body hurt all over and I never thought any more about the pain in my leg. The revealing of my leg has not fazed my mum and her expression doesn't alter, she was obviously aware of this,

19

how could she not tell me? Does she think that I already had too much to deal with?

"Oh my God, what happened to my leg? What have you done to me?" I ask the doctor looking at her in desperation. I look at Mum, I obviously look accusatory as she looks down, avoiding my gaze. "Mum, did this slip your mind?" I look at the Doctor. "How come I didn't feel this? Is there anything else I don't know?"

Dr Redmond looks at me, for the first time with a patronising expression, which I don't appreciate. "It's the sedative and local anaesthetic that we used. With the pain relief, you would have felt a dull pain, which I know you mentioned, it's in your notes, but you wouldn't have felt enough pain to isolate it to this area, thankfully. And no, there are no other surprises." She smiles and her expression is back to normal.

"What has been done? Is it my ankle or my leg? Am I going to be able to play netball and hockey? I play for my school teams, I need to get back playing, all my friends play." I feel like I am pleading now, I can hear that my tone is desperate.

"We are not sure; we need to give it at least six weeks with the rods and then a further eight weeks to recover and get strong again. Some physiotherapy will help the movement come back and with some strengthening exercises, you may be able to get back to sport but I think you need to understand that the injury was severe. There was some damage caused to your nerves and ligaments and several fractures in your left leg, ankle and foot."

My mum leans forward to hold my hand, I pull it away. How much more can I lose? Sport is my life; Jamie was my solace. Oh my God, I said *was*. Am I now accepting this? This is too much to take in. Tears are falling again.

I look at my mum, "Can I have some time on my own please?"

"Are you sure?" she asks.

"Please Mum," I reply, I look into her eyes and then down to my leg. Please leave, please leave, I am saying in my head. I don't want to say it out loud. This is not her fault, I know that, but my life is ruined.

"Okay, sweetie," she says. She grabs my hand before I can move it out of the way and squeezes it. I have brought your phone in case you want to contact your friends or keep up to date with anything going on." She hands me my phone. "It's fully charged," she says.

I take it from her and place it next to me on the bed. "Thanks, Mum."

My mum picks up her bag and stands up, scraping the chair on the tiled floor. A little embarrassed about the noise she has made, she looks up at the doctor still standing there and apologises. The doctor smiles and waves a hand in dismissal.

CHAPTER 3

Introducing Sky

Dr Redmond follows my mum to the door of the room. Before she leaves, she turns to me. "Do you have enough pain relief, Abbie?"

"Yes, thanks," I say. Enough to mask the pain in my leg that will destroy what's left of my life apparently, I think.

I watch them leave, then turn to look out of the window. How can everything keep going normally when my world is crashing down about me. It's not fair.

As I look around the room, for what feels like the hundredth time, at all of the flowers and cards, most of whom from people I don't know, I catch sight of my phone as it flashes, signalling a message has been received. I pick it up, more of a reflex action than curiosity regarding the sender or the message itself. I look at the picture on my home screen. It is me and Jamie, smiling like fools at the camera. Typically, Jamie is carrying Roger by the foot. We all knew that he was getting too old for a teddy bear and he would not carry him openly in public for fear of ridicule, but he would always have him when he was going to sleep or he had his quiet times and especially when he was going to see Karen, his child psychologist, who was helping him with his loss of dad. That's why I knew he had been in the car with Jamie during the accident.

My phone flashes again, another message, or is my phone reminding me that there is a message I hadn't opened yet? To be honest, it is impossible to check, as I had about forty messages, all unopened. I quickly scan the names of the senders: all of them are netball or hockey players and there is one from my nan. I open my nan's message first, it is dated four days ago. "Please wake up, darling. We miss you so much. We have been speaking to your mum, she's in bits. We all need you to come home." I don't realise I am crying until a tear rolls from my cheek and lands on my phone. I had forgotten about my nan and grandad until that moment. I make a mental note to text her, when I have read a few messages from my friends from school – Maidenhall High.

"Dear Abbie, we are missing you mate, so sorry about Jamie. Haven't stopped crying. He was so lovely. Please call or text me when you wake up xxx ☹ Becki." I read this and make another mental note to reply, but not yet. Becki is a good friend, I know her mainly from netball, she plays defence. Ordinarily, I wouldn't know her very well as we are from different school-houses. All of the schoolhouse names were chosen about three years ago on International Women's Day, March 8th, and are the names of influential women in recent history. I'm in Rosa Parks, Becki is in Marie Curie and there are two others, Clara Barton and Eleanor Roosevelt.

"Hi Abs, please wake up sweets. The netball pitch is quiet without you." I smile. "Seriously though, come on, we need you. Love Jess" Jess is in Rosa Parks with me. Another mental note.

"Hi Abbie, we all miss you. Saw it on the news and I was in shock, we all were. I asked when I could come to visit you, but the hospital said that they needed some more time to make sure you were ok before visitors were going to be allowed in. Can you let me know when I can come and visit and what I can bring? Speak soon, hopefully. Xxx love Sky." Sky has been my best friend for so long, since nursery, I think. We have always been in the same schoolhouse, which is part of the reason that we are so close, probably. I am surprised that she didn't mention Jamie, but I guess I am not really. He was like a brother to her too. It's probably too raw.

I decide to read some of the other messages later and reply to Sky and my Nan first.

"Dear Nan, I hope you and Grandad are okay. I think Mum is tired. The nurses have said that she has been at the hospital every day. Even though, I have only been awake for a little while. The doctor says that I am doing well, the thing in my head is getting smaller, that's a good thing. My foot is a mess though. It could be months before I do sports. I miss Jamie. I thought I heard him on the morning that I was waking up, but it was probably the sedative, that's what Mum said, and it makes sense. I wish he was here though. I hope that the police arrest the man that hit us and put him away. They should bring back hanging." I read this through and decide that it is a bit too angry for my Nan and delete everything from the, "I miss Jamie," reference. I put some kisses on the bottom, invite them to come and see me and then sign off the message.

My text to Sky was more like the original text to my Nan. I don't have to pull my punches with my friends.

"Hi Sky, thanx for the text. Only just read it. Been a nightmare here. Room stinks of flowers from people I don't know. Their cards talk about Jamie and say how much he will be missed. Seriously, how can you miss someone you never knew? FFS! How dare they! Do you know what has happened to the man who hit us? Was he arrested? He should be hanged. It's not fair. Poor Jamie. I can't believe it. My ankle is fucked. I'll probably have a limp for the rest of my life. Attractive, NOT! What about netball and hockey, my life is ruined." I read it through, and press send. I know I haven't answered her questions about visiting but I will do it later when I am a bit less cross.

I read through a few of the other messages, all of them seem very similar and the message begins to feel shallow and less heartfelt. I am sure it's not, it's just that it becomes too familiar and the repetition makes it sound insincere, even though the message has come from different senders.

I put my phone down and look out of the window. It's funny – not funny ha ha – but peculiar in a way that before this had occurred, I thought nothing of sitting for hours, looking at my phone, staring at YouTube videos, posting on Facebook and Instagram and answering messages, didn't feel tired at all but after twenty minutes of reading and replying, I'm exhausted.

I close my eyes. Immediately, I am taken back to the crash. My head is thrown to the right and then almost ricochets back. My eyes shut. I hear screaming, it's me. The sounds of the crash are deafening. Glass is everywhere. I can't see Jamie, but I know that his seat has taken the biggest impact. I can only see the crumpled mess of a wing of a car and headlight smashed outside my window. My foot is trapped by my door which has been forced in and Jamie's seat where it has been forced backwards. The pain is excruciating. There is some screeching outside, are other cars going to hit us or are they going to stop in time? Does it matter? Are we all going to die anyway?

There is a rude awakening as Mum bustles through the door. Startled, I open my eyes, grateful for the intrusion into the nightmare that has replayed each time I have succumbed to sleep.

"Oh good, you're awake, sweetie." She sits down noisily on a small chair, to my left. She opens her large, black shopping bag and produces a packet of grapes, a custard-filled Krispy Kreme doughnut. As she hands me the doughnut, I salivate. "Oh my God, Mum, that's custard?" She nods, smiling. "Thank you so much." I take a massive bite and the custard falls from the doughnut and onto my chin. Using my finger, I gather it up and scoop it into my mouth. "Umm, so amazing," I say, around the sweet bready material overwhelming my overfilled mouth.

"Slowly, sweetheart."

Mum allows me to enjoy every last morsel before speaking again.

"How are you feeling?"

"Not bad, Mum. I have read some of my messages and replied to a couple – tired me out though." I glance at my phone. Mum smile.

"Did you manage to send a message to your nan? She is so worried, beside herself."

"Yes, first one I did." I smiled, I knew that this would comfort her, especially after what I read in Nans message.

"Thanks, love." She gripped my hand, then looked instinctively at her own, obviously recognising how sticky it now was. "I was wondering if we could talk about the funeral?"

She sounded so tentative, so nervous.

"Okay, mum," It is the last thing I want to, but I know that it is what she needs to do. "What do we need to make decisions on?"

"I have ordered the coffin, an oak casket with royal blue satin lining and pillow. Are you happy with that?" she looks so vulnerable.

"Great choice, Mum. What else?" I ask. Blue was a favourite colour of his. I don't know why boys usually have favourite colours which are the same as the football team they follow. Jamie was a massive fan of Luton Town Football Club, whose colours are orange, black and white, but I never saw him in these colours apart from when he wore the team scarf I got him last Christmas. He wore it all winter.

"The music, what would he like?" She is looking down; her phone is in her hand and the notes page is open.

"I don't know, he always liked Bruno Mars when you played him, there could be an appropriate song of his. What about *Just the way you are*, it is a nice song. I know it's about a girlfriend, but I have heard him singing to it. What do you think?"

"Perfect, love. I will tell the funeral directors. What about what he should wear?"

"What about his Minecraft t-shirt?"

"I was thinking about that, good choice." I see that she is making a note on her phone. "There will need to be a reading at the ceremony, the funeral director has said that the priest is happy to do it on our behalf, but I was wondering if you would like to say something?" She looks up.

"I'm not sure I will be able to," I look at her. Our eyes meet.

"Don't worry, we don't have to decide on this yet, have a think, no pressure, honestly, love."

"When is the funeral, Mum?" I ask.

"On the twenty-seventh, in eight days' time." She says. "It's been nine days since the accident already, we need to let him rest."

I struggled to see that it had been that long, but I guess I had been in a coma for around five days, and I have been in and out of sleep since then. Today has been the most active for me, managing my messages and helping Mum with my brother's funeral arrangements. That means that accident was on the tenth.

#

Over the next few days, Dr Redmond made regular visits to my room, checking my charts, speaking briefly to me about rehabilitation and physiotherapy. As the day of the funeral draws near, I become stronger and more determined to make sure I can attend. Sky comes to see me, and we spend an hour and a half talking about everything from hockey and netball to the most attractive boys in our year, carefully avoiding any discussion about Jamie and the funeral, until she asks if I will be released for it. We both note the reference to incarceration and smile weakly.

"I hope so. The doctor knows the date and has said that she will be trying to get me there, even if it's in a wheelchair. I will have to come straight back though." I look at her.

"At least you will be there, Jamie would want you there," she says. She bites her fingernails, a habit of hers, usually when she is uncomfortable.

"I know." I nod.

The bell sounds in the main corridor of the ward, signalling the end of visiting time as they are about to serve dinner. Sky says her goodbyes and gets up to leave.

As she reaches the door, she turns around, "Get well soon, Freak head." She smiles.

I smile back at her and then watch her leave.

#

"You need to come; it's not really bye-bye you know?" I hear, not verbally, more in my head.

"Jamie... Jamie," I whisper. "Where are you?" No response. Did I hear it? Am I going mad? My head injury? The crash?

#

27th January

The day of the funeral has come. We had discussed all the options and finally decided that a cremation was going to be the choice for Jamie as he could then be scattered with dad. They could look after each other and we knew how much Jamie had missed dad since he passed; at least he would have an opportunity to be with him. It is a suitably cold and dreary day. The clouds are almost at my hospital window and the view of the motorway has thankfully been obscured by the mist and rain. The nurses are fussing more than usual. I have been given my breakfast early, about eight o'clock and Mum arrives soon after with bags of clothes for me to try on. I know I have lost a bit of weight whilst in hospital. The absence of McDonald's and Dominos has taken its toll.

I know I must wear black but beyond that, I don't know what to put on. Doctor Redmond comes into my room and asks how I feel, and whether I would like to be on crutches or in a wheelchair for the day.

I hadn't thought about this, I looked at Mum. She said that it would be easier for her if I was in a wheelchair, the ground was going to be slippery due to the rain and I may fall on crutches. The Doctor smiled and nodded. "Good thinking. I will arrange for the porter to bring one for you." She left the room.

"Mum, what will that look like? Me, in a wheelchair? Crippled. It's not fair." I feel angry at everything. The man who killed Jamie and tried to kill me and Mum, how skinny I am now, how stupid I am going to look in a wheelchair and at Jamie for leaving me. I start to cry, angry tears at first but then deflate into childish sobs.

Mum leans forward and grabs me, holding me tight. I can feel her uncontrollable sobs running through her. My forehead is wet from her tears. I pull back and get my breath. My mum looks dreadful. The whole situation has drained her.

"None of this is fair, love." She sounds exhausted, talking through shallow breaths. "We have to be here for one another. It is going to be a really tough day, lets help each other through it." She asks. She is shaking. As she looks up to me, she pulls out clothes from the bag she had brought with her. "Please try them on." She holds out a black jumper, wide leg trousers and black shoes.

"Okay, mum." I take them and look at them. Trying to smile, I pick out the left shoe and handed it back to her. "Not sure I will need this one."

She smiles and puts it back in the bag. I realise it is the first real smile since I ate the doughnut. I feel guilty for my reaction to all this. Jamie is my brother, but he was also her son. Her baby boy.

By the time I am changed behind the curtain, the porters have arrived with the wheelchair.

The priest welcomes us into the chapel and seats us at the front pew. We leave a place, as if dad was there, next to Mum. We had agreed that he was there in spirit. I manage to manoeuvre the wheelchair directly next to Mum's seat. There is also a place next to me, where I put my mums' bag. The pews behind and to the side of us fill up rapidly. People from the local community, Jamie's cub scout group, his friends from school and the obvious and unwelcomed journalists from the local paper.

I had made the decision that I wanted to say something at the funeral and after the Bruno Mars song, the priest introduces me as "Jamie's beloved sister," inviting me to come to the front, next to Jamie's coffin and say what I would like to say. Mum jumps up and pushes the chair to the front and swings me around so that I face the people there, all of whom are already crying.

"Jamie is the best brother anyone could have, he is kind, happy and funny. I love playing hide and seek with him and even though I know he peeps when it's his turn to find me, I love it." I hear Mum moan out loud at this, clearly this recollection is painful for her. I knew it would be, but I can't comfort her now. I must finish my words, for Jamie, or is it really for me? I realise that I was speaking as if he is still alive, maybe my mind-tricks and being able to hear him speaking to me, is confusing me. I decide to continue my message about Jamie in the past tense to avoid any confusion, not least my own.

"A great brother. Anyone who knew him liked him. He always saw the best in people and tried to help those in need. He had a big heart and loved easily. I will miss him."

I try to hold it together but can't help imagining him hiding behind a tree, with too much coat showing, giving away his position. Remembering the way I had to ignore the fact that I'd seen him and walk off in the opposite direction, only to hear him shout "colder" excitedly behind me.

I look up. The faces looking at me are tear-sodden and red. Tissues in many hands, and the sounds of sniffing around the chapel. I wheel myself back to my pew. Turn the chair around to face the front and take a deep breath.

"I love you, Abbie," I hear. Jamie's voice, in my head. Oh my God not here. That's not fair. I look around, why? I'm not going to see him, am I? Am I looking for the sadistic cousin with the recording of Jamie's voice? No one would do that! Idiot! I say to myself. He's not here! Well, he is, but...

#

CHAPTER 4

No Forgiveness

The priest finishes the last bible reading, something about "Walking with the hand of God, in his protection, protecting the children cruelly taken before their time," I can't help thinking that the last bit is in his own words and an addition to the original script.

We leave as the curtains pull across in front of Jamie's coffin and music plays. *Wind Beneath My Wings*, good choice. Jamie wouldn't have known it, or probably chosen to listen to it, but I know Mum and Dad had it at their wedding; we played it at dad's funeral and now for Jamie.

Did you ever know that you're my hero?
And everything I would like to be.
If I can fly higher than an eagle,
You are the wind beneath my wings...

I can't stop looking at the curtains closing, seeing the final parts of the coffin disappear as the two sides of the burgundy, velvet curtains meet. I realise that I have torn the tissue in my hands leaving only confetti in my lap. I hear myself crying and saying, "Jamie, don't leave me! Please don't go."

I look around for Mum, but she is already out of the building. This is too much for her. How do you bury a child?

I wheel the chair over the uneven square flagstones towards the medieval heavy wooden doors, where one of the doors is held open by a verger to allow me to leave unimpeded. As I travel down the short corridor to the external door, the air is getting ever chillier. I notice the flowers in the corridor for the first time. I am sure that they were in the chapel too, but I never noticed them. They were lovely, all in Jamie's favourite colours, blues and yellows. Outside, the air is cold. Mist has gathered around the wheels of my chair, making the metal rims slippery and difficult to manage. The pebbled pathway is uneven and makes the short journey I can manage on this surface uncomfortable. Although, I would not admit it, I am sure that this terrain would have been treacherous on crutches so I am glad of the security of four wheels beneath me.

"Are you ok?" A shaky, quiet voice asks from behind my chair. As the person walks into my eye line, I recognise him as a person I have seen before. I don't know him well and can't put a name to him, but I am sure it's not the first time we've met.

"Do I know you?" I ask. Almost accusatory, although I don't know why. The emotions of the day, I guess.

"Sorry, I'm Luke Harris, I was driving the car that hit you. I wanted to speak to you and tell you how sorry I am. I haven't slept since the accident. I can't live with myself. I haven't worked, can't eat. I feel so dreadful." The man looks down. He looks about twenty years old, and although he is a mess, it looks like this hasn't always been the case. Even though he appears genuine, how could he think that this would be okay? How insensitive? Just wrong.

"Please don't talk to me. My brother, my nine-year-old brother was okay before you hit us. You killed him. He is in a box because of you!" I am shouting now. Crying,

"Abbie! What are you doing? Why are you shouting? This is Jamie's day!" Mum ran over from the front of the chapel towards me, slipping on the uneven pebbles but just managing to stay upright.

She looked at Luke Harris, "What have you been saying to her, can't you see she is upset and injured, who are you?" She was cross and took on the appearance of a lioness protecting her cub, ready to pounce and defend her brood, or what was left of it.

"It's okay, Mrs Carter, I just wanted to apologise to Abbie about the accident." Luke says, he looks at Mum. When the accident is mentioned, Mum stops where she is. "What did you say? Who are you?"

"I'm sorry, I'm Luke Harris…" he clearly didn't expect to be interrupted.

"The driver of the car that hit us?" she sounded exasperated. Her hand went up to her forehead, almost like a reflexive movement, to help her brain manage the information that she had just received.

"Yes, I just wanted to apologise and try to explain…" he was pleading now.

"And you thought that today was the day to do this? I will hear you Mr Harris but not today, not here. Please leave." She looked towards the gate to the road and then back to Luke Harris. He took the hint and his head went down, defeated, and he walked slowly away.

"What do you mean, you will hear him? Mum, what could he possibly say to make this right?" I ask in disbelief.

"We all make mistakes, Abbie, some are small, others are tragic, but they are all accidents. We are all human, none of us is perfect and sometimes forgiveness needs to be an option to help everyone work through the pain…

Anger hurts. Would Jamie want you to hurt for any longer than is really necessary?" She reaches for my hand, leans forward and kisses my cheek, which is still running with the tears of frustration and sadness.

"I can't forgive him, Mum. Jamie's gone and it's his fault." I tell her. I watch him as he gets to the road and turns left out of the chapel grounds. He doesn't look back.

#

When the rest of the congregation has left the chapel and we have said our goodbyes, Mum phones the hospital to arrange for the patient transport to take me back. She was grateful for the excuse not to have a wake for Jamie as she was completely exhausted from the day.

The ambulance only takes minutes to get to the chapel. They drive up the in-out driveway and stop at the front door. Two transport workers get out of the ambulance, lower the platform at the rear and push my wheelchair on to it. As it is now rush hour on a cold January afternoon, it seems to take so long to get back to the ward.

For the next two weeks, I spend most of the time either in my bed, bored out of my head or working through my physiotherapy and all the excruciating pain with a sergeant major physiotherapist. Sky comes and sees me most days and when she can't come, she texts me. We catch up on the news from school, who is seeing who, who is in the school hockey and netball teams in my place and how well or badly they are doing. I know that she has my interests at heart and will tell me the truth, probably the only one of my friends who really would. I know that Zoe, from Eleanor Roosevelt, who has always been my deputy and itched for my captain's armband, will take my place and probably do well. I just hope that the physiotherapy works, and I can get back soon enough, before she becomes part of the furniture.

I tell Sky about Luke Harris. She had been at the funeral, but he had left the grounds before she had come out of the chapel. I didn't tell her on the day, I was so upset. As I tell her, she looks a bit strange, like she knows something I don't.

"What?" I say, annoyed that she doesn't seem as angry as I am.

"Well," she says. She looks uncomfortable. "What he did was unforgiveable, we all know that, Abbie. It's just that, we were talking at school about the accident and how it happened. There's more to it that you probably don't know, because you were stuck in the hospital, but he wasn't just driving badly and crashed into you, his sister goes to our school, Gemma Harris. She's a first year, in Marie Curie. She has been talking about what went on just before he crashed into you."

"Well, what did she say?" I sound cross and impatient. What could possibly have happened to excuse what happened?

"She said that he had just been told that his brother, their brother, had been killed. He was a soldier, fighting in Afghanistan. They were really close before his brother had joined the army and he always looked up to him. He wasn't in his right mind when he got in the car. She said that he hasn't slept since the accident, he feels so guilty. All he talks about is what he has done to you and Jamie." Sky looks at me, that penetrating stare that tells me to think about what I want to say before I say it.

I want to stay angry, I am angry, but am I also feeling sorry for him? How can I feel both? Surely, they are opposite feelings? This is too hard.

I don't know what to say. "Mum said at the funeral that she would be happy to meet him. I don't think I am ready to do that," I tell her.

"You don't have to, but it might help you to stop being angry and concentrate on getting better?" she grabs my hand. "I don't know how Zoe is going to do but she won't be a patch on you and if you don't hurry up and get back on the teams, we are in danger of losing our place in the league."

"No pressure then?" I smile. "Actually, they are letting me out in a few days, they said. I can't wait. Get to my own bed, get back to school. I need things to be normal."

"I think you're right," she says. She leans forward and gives me a hug. "Remember what I said, try not to be angry, it will eat you up. You will miss Jamie, God, we all will, but I don't think he would want you to stay angry. That wasn't his way. He looked for the good in people, you know that." She smiles, weakly.

I nod and am still nodding as she picks up her bag to leave the room.

"See you later, Abbie."

"Later, thanks for coming." I watch her leave and then turn to the window. I can see the motorway clearly today. It is not as misty as it was on the day of the funeral. The cars streaming in either direction, drivers and passengers seemingly without a care in the world, whilst my world has been turned upside down.

#

CHAPTER 5

Back to School

It was three days later that I was allowed home. On the first of February, I left my private room on Ruby ward in St Matthews Hospital. This had been my "home" for twenty-one days. Due to my intensive physiotherapy with the sergeant major, I was able to limp successfully, using my crutches for balance rather than support. Mum was fussing around me, explaining that she had bought in all my favourite foods and had actually made a chocolate cake for after dinner. I seriously can't remember the last homemade chocolate cake I had.

We are driven down the high street, towards our road by patient transport. I see the people through the ambulance windows are shopping, eating sandwiches on benches and carrying on with their lives as if nothing has changed. For them, nothing has, I guess.

"Almost there, Abbie, be strong." Jamie's voice in my head. I don't look round. I know it is just the stress of the situation, going back to the house, where he will never be again. I am strong, I think to myself, I can do this.

"I know you can, Abbie. I am with you."

I get through the front door and into the living room. It's a bit chilly and I shiver. The hospital room was always kept warm and additional blankets were available to keep out the draft from the antiquated window shutters. Our house seemed less friendly than it used to, empty, heartless and far too quiet.

"I'll put the heating on again, it has been on already but as we waited so long for transport, it's gone off and the place has cooled down. It won't take long to warm up again. Would you like me to get you a jumper? What about the lovely Victoria Secret one I got you for Christmas? You love that." Mum is fussing and talking so fast it's difficult to keep up with her.

"A jumper would be good, Mum, thanks," I say.

I only have to wait for a couple of days, and I'm able to go back to school. I know Mum has been to see the teachers and head to arrange for me to return. Most of my lessons are on the ground floor anyway so the only issue is using crutches in the crowds of schoolkids who would be in the corridors at the beginning and end of school and in between lessons. It's not the first time that students have used crutches at school so they are well practiced at releasing kids early out of lessons so they can have a head start on the rush.

The weekend before school was the longest two days of my life. Mum wouldn't leave me alone, when that was exactly what I wanted and needed. It was infuriating. Thankfully I had my phone and Sky came down.

I spent the whole time in my room, if Sky was at mine, she was with me, if she wasn't, I was on Skype to her or text or Snapchat, either way we were chatting. I am sure Mum is just trying to replace Jamie with me, but I am not him.

#

I arrange with Sky to meet at the bottom of the big hill the morning of 4th February, my first day back to school. Big hill is a large grassy hill which, although steep, and almost impassable in the summer due to the incredibly long and tangled grasses, provides a shortcut to all the

Maidenhall High School pupils living on our side of it, cutting around fifteen minutes off our school commute should we consider walking around it.

At the top of the big hill is a large building. It is incredibly old, grey and dilapidated. I am sure it has been grand in the past but that must be in the dim and distant past. I don't know what the building once was for sure, but it is now not believed to be inhabited, at least, not by anyone alive. There is a story that it was a stately home for someone rich but then it was loaned to the war effort and injured soldiers were housed and taken care of there. After that, it became a mental hospital for the criminally insane, but these are all local myths and I don't know if there are any truths amongst them. Currently, there is a woman who is supposed to live in the old house, she is clothed all in white and she is believed to take children, like the child-catcher in the Chitty Chitty Bang Bang story. No one can confirm who this woman is or was or if she is supposed to be alive or long since deceased. Parents of the area are even known to threaten their children with the "white lady" when they misbehave.

The mysteries regarding this house are urban legends and all the kids of the area are afraid of the building and its surroundings which is why, when using the hill as a shortcut for school, the house is given a wide berth.

"R U ready?" I text to Sky. "YT?" We were well-practiced in using shortcuts in our texts to save the milliseconds it would take to write the messages properly. YT (you there?) was one that was often used in the morning. It served the added purpose of allowing our messages to remain a secret, even if either of our parents were to snoop into our phones.

"Yep here, where U?" she replies.

"I'm here," I say, as I walk up behind her. I'm surprised that she hasn't heard my crutches on the ground as I reach her until I see her take out her headphones as she turns around.

"I thought you'd be a lot longer on those," she says and smiles. "Shall we go?"

"Yes, lets." I feel nervous, I didn't know why, I guess I am expecting to be treated like an animal in a zoo, people feeling sorry for me, people who didn't even know Jamie.

We make our way to the big hill. Luckily, the rain and mist had disappeared as I think that the damp ground may have been slippery under the rubber bungs at the bottom of my crutches. We made our way around the bottom of the hill, not even attempting the elevation. It makes the journey slightly longer, but it means that I'm able to use my crutches, we are able to stay away from the big house and still cut time off the journey.

My phone pings, indicating a message. I have to stop, lean on one of the crutches, lean the other one on the one I am leaning on and get my phone out of my pocket. I look at my screen.

"It's from Jess," I tell Sky.

"U at Sch 2day?" the message reads.

"Yes, CYAL8R" I reply. (See you all later)

I put my phone back in my pocket, making a mental note not to answer it whilst I am on my crutches again. Too much faff and takes too long.

"You'll be fine, Freak head" a small voice in my head, Jamie's voice. I am finding this comforting now. I know it's probably my own mind playing tricks but it's nice to have him with me, not really gone. I decide not to tell

Sky about Jamie and him talking to me. I trust Sky but I am afraid that she may think that I am losing it, hearing voices as a result of the trauma, or just plain, going mad. I like the idea of keeping him as my secret. Something that we can continue to share, no one can take that away.

The journey to school is the longest walk I have done on my crutches and although my palms are beginning to hurt and get hot due to the way I am gripping the handles, I feel a lot more confident on them by the time we reach the school. Negotiating slippery pathways and pavement curbs have made my shoulders and wrists tense but I seem to have developed skills none of us know we have until we have to use them.

As I approach the main school entrance doors a commanding voice bellows from the school office, "Miss Carter, come here please." The school receptionist, Miss Wilson stands behind her desk, leaning on her hands and looking over her glasses which are perched on the end of her nose. She is one of those people who has become much older than her years. I would put her about thirty-five, but she really does act like a fifty-year-old woman with lots of cats and I know that if your ball was to go into her garden she wouldn't give it back to you, which is my usual indicator of a good person.

"Miss Carter, if you could wait here please, I have arranged for you to be escorted to your lessons." It doesn't seem much of a request, more command.

"Can't Sky stay with me, she's in all of my lessons and she doesn't mind." Sky shakes her head to agree. "It seems silly to have someone else with us."

"Rules are rules, Miss Carter. An agreement was signed up with your mother." She holds up a piece of paper and flapped it in my direction. "This is how it must be." She points to the adjacent, moulded grey plastic chair, which sits as a set of three strewn together with a tube of steel running between and beneath them. Not comfortable but easily washable and resilient to the damage inflicted by many teenagers determined to cause havoc.

Defeated, I sit down.

"See you in science, first period." Sky says. She smiles and walks through the internal door towards the corridor which leads to the classrooms.

"Miss Slater," Sky looks at Miss Wilson, "I don't think that I have heard the school bell yet, as you are fully aware, this means that you need to follow your other school mates and walk around the outside of the building to the playground and wait to be allowed in the main building." Her outstretched hand and boney index finger indicates the way that she wishes for Sky to go.

I smile, there is only three minutes to go, but Miss Wilson is known to be a stickler for the rules and uncompromising under any circumstances, so this is expected.

"But it's freezing out there and there are only a few minutes to go, please." Sky is really laying the pleading on thick, but Miss Wilson is unyielding.

"Less time to suffer the cold then, anyway, it's hardly Siberia. Off you go, away with you." She flaps her hand in dismissal, almost like she is trying to shake off an annoying fly and looks down to the paperwork on her desk.

Despondent, Sky leaves, with a half-hearted wave to me. The automatic door opens to allow her exit then closes as she leaves the building. Where I sit, I can just about take advantage of the heat streaming from the heater above the main doors which was designed, by shape and location, to make the entrance of the school more appealing to those entering from the blistering cold outside. I could completely understand why Sky is reluctant to return to the biting wind of this early winter morning.

Within minutes of Sky leaving, the bell signalling the start of morning lessons sounds. I watch those for whom the bell is really a starting pistol and indicates their need to run from the school gates in order to reach the front doors, via the playground before being labelled late and in receipt of a detention slip. These dedicated runners are in stark contrast with those who are not affected by the bell at all. They don't look up and nor do they quicken their step. Their silent rebellion is obvious as I watched their determined expressions of defiance.

#

"Are you Abbie?" a short first year girl asks, looking down at me.

I look at her incredulously, I think better of saying, "Do you think? What was your brief, look for the girl with pins in her leg and crutches, seriously?" Instead, I take a deep breath and think that she is probably nervous, and I just say, "Yes, what's your name?"

"Stacy, I'm to take you to your lessons today." She looks at me as if this is the biggest inconvenience. I don't blame her; I would hate it.

"I tried to get them to allow my friend to see me through the corridors, but they wouldn't have it," I explain.

"Don't worry, its okay," she says.

We allow the bustling, heaving crowds to disperse into their various classrooms, until there are just the uninterested dawdlers left to block my view and my way to lab four. Stacy tolerantly waits for several them to make their way through the corridor. A big mistake having a first year lead me around. I am a little more impatient than she is and have the confidence to impress on them the need to move out of my way.

"Coming through, make way!" I shout as I clip an ankle or two with my crutches.

"Oi, watch what you're doing." They look around, indignantly. Their speed doesn't change although their direction does alter slightly.

We arrive at lab four and agree to meet just after class so that she can lead me to maths, which is my lesson just before break. It is the only one of my lessons that is located upstairs so I am not looking forward to negotiating the staircase against the flow of traffic as the downward rush is always quicker and more forceful than those ascending. Stacy opens the door for me, and I immediately look through the open space to find Sky. I see her at the back of the classroom, she motions for me to join her and I see a space beside her. I turn my head to see the teacher at the front of the class and he nods solemnly at me, raising his hand to indicate for me to join Sky at her table.

"Some diseases can be treated with antibiotics. The vaccinations provided allow protection against specific diseases, but of course, the level of protection depends chiefly on the amount of people vaccinated…" Mr Luxford is saying. The class was clearly discussing vaccinations and epidemics whilst I had been away and my entrance into the classroom stopped the flow of his delivery. Although he had been courteous on my arrival, he is quick to pick up where he had left off. The consummate professional.

There is a slide of a small black boy, around three years old, painfully thin and a woman holding him, she wears a very thin materialled wide scarf around her painfully skinny body and draped over her head, to shield her from the blistering sun. The material fails to mask the cheekbones, evidence of malnutrition and disease. The picture is indication of the stark reality of the Ebola crisis in Africa. So incredibly sad.

Mr Luxford asks questions regarding the outbreak, how we think it could have been prevented, how and why we should do more. The class join in the discussion, half-heartedly. Clearly an emotive topic which we, fourteen-year-old school pupils in Luton, will have no chance of influencing. However, you have to commend his enthusiasm in attempting to encourage us to think we could.

"Uplifting," Sky says ironically, as we are leaving. We had to wait for everyone else to have left the room prior to us making our way to the door, to allow my safe passage.

Mr Luxford calls over, "Abbie," and motions for me to hobble over to his desk.

"Sir?" I managed to negotiate the tightly-positioned science benches with difficulty as I make my way towards him.

"I am so sorry about your brother and everything. It must be dreadful for you and your family." He looks concerned. Who knows what to say at times like this?

"Thanks, sir. It is." I don't know what to say either. We look at each other for a short time and then the discomfort of the situation overwhelms us and we both look away.

I see Stacy waiting outside the room. "My minder is here, I'll see you in maths," I tell Sky. "Can you let Mr Dawson know why I'm going to be late?"

"Yeah, sure." She secures her bag on her left shoulder and walks over to the door. "See you in a minute." Sky leaves and joins the chaos in the corridor. I wait, just inside the science lab with the door open. Stacy steps in the room with me and we wait for the crowds to dwindle before braving the journey up the stairs to the maths zone.

It is whilst we are on our way to the maths corridor that I see the notice board at the foot of the staircase. I had never noticed it before, can't believe I missed it.

"Is this new?" I ask Stacy, pointing at the two metre square, blue felt pin board.

She looks at the board and smiles, "Yes, it went up about three weeks ago. The teachers were all saying that we weren't reading the letters or newsletters that they gave us and so they wanted to have something on show and to make us want to read it, we are allowed to put up our own notices as well as theirs." She shook her head. "There have been some really nasty things put up there that had to be taken down pretty quick but it's never before most of the school have seen them. That's where they put the newspaper cutting about your crash." She looks down, her hand had grasped for the solid wooden stair rail, which scalloped at the bottom of the stairs and her right foot had taken the first step, although her weight had not yet transferred. She tentatively waits for my response.

"So, everyone knows?" I ask quietly.

"I guess so, it's the main corridor and I guess that anyone who didn't read it would have heard others talk about it." She takes the step. "We need to go, you'll be late."

"Who put the cutting up there? A teacher?" I couldn't think why a teacher would put a cutting on the notice board, but maybe they could have just been doing it in a weird way, as a mark of respect for Jamie and me. So that the other kids knew and then didn't ask any stupid questions. But wouldn't they need our permission first? Mum wouldn't have allowed it though. I know she wouldn't. She knows I like to be private. We had all of the trolls and horrible messages after dad died, we wouldn't want to go through that again. I don't think I could go through that again.

"I don't think so, they were cross and took it down straight away. I don't think they wanted you to have that sort of attention." She says, now three or four steps ahead of me as I haven't moved from the notice board. She turns around and notices I haven't followed her.

"Who then?" I ask. I have my suspicions, but it seems cruel and extreme for even her.

"It's only a rumour but I know that a girl called Tracy was mentioned but I don't know anything else and I haven't got anything to back that up." She looks at her watch and as she looked up at me, her face is one of concern. "Come on, I am supposed to make sure you get to class. The teacher will be wondering where you are, and I will get in trouble."

I nod and start up the stairs. I had thought that the cow who would have done that would have been Tracy Parsons. A new low. Why would anyone do that? I feel so exposed. It was okay to hobble around on my crutches but to have the worst day of my life plastered on the school wall. They probably knew anyway but not necessarily. Most of these kids have their heads in PlayStation and Snapchat as soon as they get home, so may not have known about the accident and about Jamie and thanks to Tracy, now they do. An animal in the zoo....

CHAPTER 6

Replaced

It's not until after maths that I have an opportunity to speak to Sky. Did she know about the notice board and the cutting? Why didn't she tell me if she did know? I make a mental note to ask Stacy to meet me after lunch to take me to the afternoon classes but would assure her that Sky can take me to break and then on to art as the studio was adjacent to the playground.

We work through the mystery that is quadratic equations. I don't know if it is maths or a foreign language class, either way, I leave the classroom confused and with less understanding than when I went in. Maths is beyond me; you have to know when you're beaten. Stacy comes to the classroom but agrees to meet me after lunch. She looks relieved and quickly makes her way to the playground to find her friends, who, due to her babysitting duties, she has probably not seen all day.

Sky waits with me in the classroom for the corridor and stairs to clear sufficiently for me to attempt the stairs with the confidence of reaching the bottom, still standing. She leaves the room every few minutes to check the flow of kids from the various maths classrooms on this corridor and the English lessons, which also feeds into the stairway traffic. After her third venture beyond the door, she returns, smiling.

"Are you ready? It's pretty clear now."

"Yes, sure."

We make our way down the gradually rounded staircase. I remain on the right side as it is the widest part of the stairs, and Sky dutifully walks beside me, steadying me on a couple of occasions when my crutches go slightly wayward.

As we reach the bottom of the stairs, I stop and look at the notice board.

"You wouldn't have seen this would you? It went up when you were in the hospital. Teachers thought we needed it to make sure we read the notices they were giving us, and they have said that we can put up our own. So, there are invites to swim meets, the hockey, football, rugby and netball fixtures go up there and other stuff, like lost dogs, you know the type of thing…" she trails off. "It's a good idea, don't you think? I never read any of the letters they gave us, but I do read this, it's kind of eye-catching, more relevant." She stops again.

"Does anyone check stuff before it's pinned up there? Any of the teachers, you know, in case its cruel or nasty?" I ask. I think that my question makes it quite obvious what I am thinking but I do wonder if she is going to go there.

"Are you talking about the newspaper cutting?" she asks. I nod slowly. I look at her, she looks uncomfortable, like she has been found out in a lie.

"I am so sorry, Abbie. I wanted to tell you, but you were already nervous about coming in and I didn't want to make you worry about what people knew or thought they knew. It was put up and taken down within the hour on the same day and that was weeks ago. Who told you?"

"It was Stacy, she said it was someone called Tracy. Was that Tracy Parsons?" I ask, already knowing the answer.

"Yes, I think so. That's what I heard." She shakes her head. "What a bitch, how could anyone be that hideous?"

"When has she been any different? Her dad drives around in a Lexus. Her mum doesn't have to work. She goes on all the school trips and has new stuff all the time, going to concerts at the O2, what can I do? What have we got? She has always taken the piss out of me, my old clothes, second-hand books and uniform, it's not fair. You'd think that she would leave some things alone though, wouldn't you? Just have an ounce of respect, for Jamie if not for me?" I am starting to get upset and I really don't want to. The kids are coming in from break now and I need to get to Art before the corridors are impassable. "I doesn't matter," I say dismissively, both me and Sky know it really does. "Come on, let's go."

We make our way to the art studio, which sits next to the playground, overlooking the netball pitch outline on the tarmac. We arrive just before the mass crowd comes into the corridor from the playground in response to the bell indicating the end of break time. Our art teacher, Mrs Allen, ushers both of us into the classroom and indicates seats on the front row for us to sit in. We dutifully make our way to them as Mrs Allen opens the door and twenty-five other pupils pour in from the corridor, all bustling through the small door opening with bags and continuing conversations, long since important, and no longer being listened to.

#

Lunch in the main hall feels quite ordinary apart from the crutches, which seem to be in the way wherever I put them.

"Don't worry," Sky reassures me. She's already made two trips to the food counter to get our lunches and water, bringing them back on separate trays, laying them down in front of me.

My left ankle is killing me, and I have had enough. "I'm going home soon," I tell Sky.

She nods and says, "Okay, if you're sure. We only have one more lesson this afternoon. Do you want me to come with you?"

"Alright, Hop-along!" I hear from behind me, at the same moment as my right shoulder is thrown forward with a force from something or someone pushing into me. I wince and turn quickly to see Tracy Parsons laughing down at me, clearly ridiculing me to show off in front of her hideous friends. "No more netball for you, freak! We don't have space for any cripples on the team. Zoe is brilliant, can't believe we put up with a loser like you for so long!" She lets out a derisive laugh to the joy of her sycophantic friends and walks past my crutches, which are leaning against the canteen wall. Trailing her foot, she pulls the crutches away from the wall, causing them to slip down the smooth, wipeable surface and clatter to the floor, drawing the attention of most of the other hungry students in the hall.

I feel mortified. Everyone is looking around. There is nowhere to hide.

"What a bitch!" says Sky. "Don't worry, Abbie."

"That's it, I'm leaving. You can come if you want, I'm going home." I tell Sky. Tears are welling in my eyes and the last thing I want to do is to give Tracy or her freaky friends the satisfaction that they have upset me. I stand, with a lot of difficulty, pulling my left leg out from underneath the canteen table and leave my untouched lunch on the surface. My appetite is lost.

Sky stands quickly and runs over to my crutches and retrieves them for me. As she hands them to me, she looks at me and says, "I am sorry, mate, I can come with you to the office, to get your mum to come or to get a taxi but I shouldn't leave school really. I have four topics to do on my course work for science, I'm behind and need to catch up, although, if you really need me to, I will. I will meet you at the bottom of the hill in the morning though, if you're coming to school tomorrow. Just text me or call me tonight and we will sort it then."

"I'm with you, Abbie," Jamie's voice. I know we had his funeral, but it is so comforting to have him with me.

"Why are you here?" I ask him, in my head.

"I never left you," he replies

"Yeah okay," I tell Sky. We leave the canteen and head towards the office. We pass under the maths staircase, walking carefully on the slippery tiled floor and past the large noticeboard. As I hobble past this, I look up and immediately notice something different pinned to this blue board. I move closer to the announcement form so I could read it. "The netball fixtures… next match against St Josephs on 6th February…Zoe in the Centre position." I read the notice thoroughly. "I am not even on the list, not even down as injured and there is nothing on there that says who Zoe is replacing or that it's temporary. It's like I never existed." I am annoyed. "It's like I died, not Jamie."

"Oh my God, Abbie… it's more likely to be a typo, don't you think? For fuck's sake, you need to get perspective on this. If it's about Tracy and her shitty friends, that's one thing but this is a massive shift from missed off the fixture list to not existing at all…" Sky sound like she was despairing with me.

We are quiet for the rest of our journey to the office. We both need to have a little cooling-off period. When we get to the office, Sky sits on the uncomfortable plastic seat just outside reception, looking at the floor. I don't think she wants to look at me. I am too angry to see this from any other perspective than my own. Sky should have been as annoyed as me, couldn't she see how unfair this was?

I lean against the reception desk and wait for Miss Wilson to come from the back room. I can hear the kettle boiling and then a cup being stirred with a metal spoon against porcelain. I lean my crutches against the wooden reception shelf and put all my weight on my right foot. My left leg is throbbing, and I feel exhausted, although I don't think it is only my injury that is making me feel so tired.

Miss Wilson walks through the connecting door, holding a steaming cup. "Oh Miss Carter, is there a problem?" she looks as concerned as I have ever seen her look, in short, not very concerned at all. "Miss Carter…well? Well?" Back to being impatient – the Miss Wilson we all recognise.

"I am really tired, and my leg hurts a lot, I really need to go home. Can you ring my mum please?"

"I will try, Miss Carter." She picks up the phone on the desk but as she is keying in the first three numbers she looks up and spots Sky sitting on the chair, watching our conversation. "Miss Slater, what are you doing here? Can I do anything for you?"

"No, Miss Wilson, I'm here with Abbie." She nods in my direction.

"Off you go then, Miss Slater." She waves her away, towards the internal corridor.

Sky takes the hint. "I'll call you or text you later, Abbie." She walks away, barely looking at me.

"Okay. Later."

"Your mum is on her way, Miss Carter." Miss Wilson motions to the seats that Sky has just vacated, and I sit down. I put my crutches through two seats to stop them from falling to the floor, leaning the top of them against the wall of the reception area.

Mum arrives about ten minutes later, in the courtesy car loaned to us by the insurance company. Our own car was so damaged in the accident that we were told that it would take weeks to repair. In the meantime, we are using a Seat Leon. It feels very similar to our old car, but it is a newer model and is a little bigger inside, which makes it much easier to deal with my crutches. I had never smelt the 'new car' smell but now I know what people mean when they talk about it. It does feel special. During the journey, Mum clearly wants to talk and attempts conversation several times, but I huff and stare out of the window. My leg hurts a lot but that isn't really the most important thing on my mind right now. What had I expected? Everyone to be nice to me? Tracy Parsons to have a personality transplant and stop being a bitch? Sky to understand and support me?

CHAPTER 7

Someone to Talk To

When we get home, I struggle out of the front seat of the car and start hobbling up the flagstone pathway to the door.

"Abbie, I was thinking…" Mum is trying again. I turn to look at her. I need to get in the house and sit down, rest my leg, but she is obviously going to want me to listen to her.

"What, what is it?" I know that this has come out a little more impatient than I expected. She looks hurt.

"I have been thinking," she says quietly. "How would you feel about talking to someone? Someone who can discuss the accident, Jamie and… your dad even? I have done some checking and there is an agency where they deal with childhood bereavement, all their clients are between twelve and eighteen. Its linked to the local Hospice and they would welcome you, should you wish to go. They would be happy to arrange sessions on the same days as your physiotherapy appointments so that you don't have to have any more time off school." She looks nervous as she looks up. "What do you reckon? Would you give it a go? It might help. If it doesn't, we can cancel it."

"I don't think I need it but if you want me to go, if you think I'm crazy, I'll go," I say, still fuming from the day's events. I really thought that I would get some support from home. From Mum, my only family now.

"Karen helped me, Abbie, it will make mummy happy." I hear Jamie's voice. "Please try it, I want you to be happy."

Jamie's voice takes me by surprise. I am getting used to hearing him, but this is too relevant to what is going on to be a fluke of my mind. If his voice is my own creation, why would I try and convince myself to do something I definitely don't want to do? "Okay, mum," I say reluctantly. I imagine Jamie smiling.

"What, you'll go?" she is ecstatic. "I'll arrange it, oh thanks, Abbie. I love you so much."

#

For nine weeks I have got to attend bereavement counsellor sessions. My counsellor is called Dave and is around mid-thirties, overweight and from the north; Yorkshire, I think. He sounds like people in Emmerdale Farm on the TV – not that I've watched it, but I've heard the accent. We have met every two weeks for the last month and I feel like I am going around in circles. The first week was painful, I just didn't want to be there, and had it not been for Jamie sitting on my shoulder, pleading with me to give it a go, I would have walked out within the first few minutes.

I had to describe myself to Dave, not necessarily my feelings, that came later, but who I was, what I did and what I wanted to be. He didn't seem to understand that that had all changed. Who I was before the accident was not who I am now, nor is what I do as I can't do what I could before and as for what I want to be, does it matter? Things change so quickly, I could have a plan, a dream and it would all be quashed because some idiot running away from reality choses to wipe you out with no whys or wherefores and WHAM you have no life, no future. What is the point in planning or wishing? I'm sure Jamie had dreams. In fact, I know he did. He wanted to be an astronaut or a doctor and, on some days, a police officer, like dad.

As the weeks go on, I open up more and tell Dave that I am tired of the feeling that I should not be here. Why was I saved when my brother died? I tell him, as he didn't know Jamie, how great he was, annoying at times, like all brothers but I loved him. I didn't realise how much I really cared about him until he wasn't there anymore. Dave asks about my mum, and how I feel about her. This is difficult to answer. I was definitely a daddy's girl and I know that Mum was probably hoping that when she had me, that I was going to be 'her little girl', pigtails and ballet shoes, but I couldn't be that. I was more, climbing trees and riding bikes. A big disappointment to her from the word go. I remember my dad calling me, 'his princess', ironic really as I never behaved like a princess, but our relationship was unbreakable. He meant the world to me. As always, whenever anyone asks about my mum, I end up talking about my dad, a much more comfortable place for me. Comfortable that is, until we get to the point where he died.

We talk about school, about my lessons, my favourite lessons, sports, and the relationships I have with the kids at school. I talk about my loss of place on the netball team, my relationship with Tracy Parsons, how horrible she has always been and the fact that she had put the newspaper clipping on the notice board. My fight with Sky, what Sky had said, how she didn't see things from my point of view and how I reacted. How Zoe had played at the netball match on the sixth of February and how unlikely it was that I would be able to earn my place back, especially with the fact that I was now a cripple. We discuss my injury and I explain that the physiotherapy is going well but the physiotherapist has told me that I would never have the strength in my left foot and ankle to compete again. I have lost so much. Everything that means anything to me.

Dave listens to me talk each time we met. He nods at the right places and leaves silences, so I feel that I have to fill them. We talk about how I'm feeling. We talk about the stages of grief and how I feel I am supported. I explain that I feel numb about everything but oddly, I find myself trying to defend Mum. She had never encouraged me to talk about my dad or Jamie. As soon as dad's funeral was finished, she disappeared into herself and couldn't help me because she couldn't help herself. It has been similar with Jamie's death, the only difference being that she won't let me breathe without her knowing it, won't let me out of her sight. Like she doesn't want to be left alone, not that she loves me more, it doesn't feel like that. More her needs than mine. I am still so angry. I don't tell him that Jamie had been speaking to me, that's my business and the only thing keeping me going. I don't want to be analysed or for him to question if I am mad or not because I am hearing my dead brother's voice.

Based on what I had told him, Dave explains that what I am feeling is completely normal. He says that he would expect me to feel angry. That my feelings matter and that I should work through them. I can't see a way to do this as Mum won't talk to me, and I can't talk to her without her walking out of the room. Dave suggests that I keep a diary, write down my feelings when stuff happens at home or school. He hands me a day per page diary. I've never had a diary before, it always seemed lame, a bit stupid, and I couldn't see how writing down how I was feeling would help but I say I will fill it in when I can.

My physiotherapy is difficult and painful. My limp is a constant reminder of the accident and my continuing inability to get back what I had. Whatever we try, I just can't build enough strength in my ankle to run or even jog. Each time I put my foot down in more than a walk, I wince in pain.

Since losing my crutches about five weeks ago, getting around school has been a lot easier. Stacy was able to go back to her friends and although she never said so, I know she was pleased to be relieved of the minder role she had and could get to her own classes in time. Tracy Parsons has continued to dog me around school, even trying to trip me up at every opportunity. Even at home, I'm not safe from her as she has posted direct messages to my Instagram account, laughing at my leg and me generally. I screenshot some of her messages.

'Who do you think you are? No one cares about you.'

'Big-shot in the paper. Don't make me laugh. Stupid, cripple and ugly.'

'Always rubbish at netball, thank God the accident happened, and we can have a decent player. A chance to win at last.'

'Forever alone, no one will ever want to go out with someone with special shoes.'

There are others but I can't believe how much they affect me. I try not to read them but can't help it. I think about blocking her but sometimes it's better to know what people are thinking. At least these were sent to me, and although I would not sleep at night once I read them and wonder whether they were actually true and people really did think I was a loser, is anyone else reading them. It is after the session with Dave where we discuss the diary that I decide to try writing down my feelings regarding the posts to see if I can deal with them and what they're doing to me.

Date: April 4th

Went to school, struggling to deal with the Trolls on Instagram ☹ WTF am I supposed to do? Can't cope. Can't run, such a cripple. What's the fucking use of me? Maybe the Trolls are right!? I'm struggling to eat. Don't seem to need to, no appetite. Mum hassling me about it. I can't sleep, just keep going back to the accident when I try. Not telling Mum. Don't need any more grief. Sky came around today, we watched YouTube videos, had a laugh. Told her about the Inst posts from Bitch-head but she said not to worry. No one likes her anyway and she's just jealous. Maybe she's right? I don't think so though.

Date: April 5th

Shit day at school today, BH tripped me in the main hall when we went into assembly. Flat on my face, leg burned. Everyone laughed. Jamie told me not to worry.

I erase this entry in case Dave wants to read my diary. I know its private, but that doesn't mean that he won't want to read it, Jamie is my business, not his.

Preparation for school exams begin properly after Easter break, and we are all expected to complete revision in addition to our homework, which of course, doesn't cease during this period. I try to keep up my diary entries, but it isn't as easy. I feel the need to study hard as I missed so much in hospital and never really caught up. Sky is helping me and the fact that we are in the same classes for everything makes it a bit easier as she has always been good at taking notes, which comes in really handy. We meet together, with our books during every break time, after lunch and she comes around after school.

"Such a swot, why bother? What a loser!" I hear the dulcet tones of Tracy Parsons from the maths zone corridor when she sees us both in the maths room during break, taking advantage of the solitude as most of the students are on the playground and try to get our heads around the decimal to fraction conundrum. "Sitting with your girlfriend, again, loser? So that's why no boys will go near you? Not just because you are so ugly" her friends laugh. They continue to do the wheezy giggle behind their hands as I reply.

"Piss off, go and bully a first year," I say this as a dismissal and turn to Sky in an effort to continue what we were doing and ignore her.

"You'll regret that, loser. Seriously, don't talk to me like that, who the hell do you think you are?" She pushes Andrea Green, one of her friends, in the middle of her back, away from the door and they all walk down the corridor. As they leave, I worry about what she said, as Tracy has the capacity to make my life a nightmare, and it is the first time I have ever bitten back. I can see that it came as a surprise to Sky, so I am not shocked with the reaction from Tracy and her cronies. I don't know what she will do, attack me? I can't defend myself with my stupid leg.

I look at Sky, and we look down at the books, with the intention of continuing with wading through decimal points and all the other boring parts to them when the school bell, indicating the end of breaktime, comes to our rescue.

We pack our books away in our bags and make our way down the maths corridor and down the stairs to the atrium so we can make our way to the art studio. There is a steady swarm of pupils moving up the stairs, me and Sky are struggling against the tide. I look down towards the bottom of the stairs and see the notice board on ground level. There is a note on the board, which I had not seen when we made our way up the stairs for our breaktime study session. My attention is drawn as it is so colourful but from where I am I can't make out what it is.

I am walking normally now, thankfully, although I know that it is sometimes noticeable that I favour my right leg and walking down the stairs with so many people walking in the opposite direction, testing my confidence in making it down to the ground floor. As we make our way down, it is clear that a note on the board had attracted the interest of those due to be ascending. A small crowd has gathered and there is a little muttering and giggling. As we pass the notice board, a distinct pathway through the crowd to the notice board seems to form allowing us to stand in front of the board. When there, my attention is drawn to something colourful underneath the sports fixtures. I locate the notice that had attracted my attention at the top of the stairs and I see a white piece of paper which had clearly been written on by someone in a rush. There was a large red heart drawn around the centre of the paper. In the heart were four capital letters, written in black, with a add sign separating the first two from the second two. AC + SS. The words FOREVER IN LOVE were written in black, underneath the red heart shape. I tear this piece of paper off the notice board and screw it up and put it in my bag. I am so angry. It is clear who has written it and that it is referring to me and Sky. I look at Sky and know I am probably overreacting to this, certainly Sky's expression makes me think that she might think that I am over the top.

"I'm sorry, Sky. Things make me angry, I guess I overreacted. It has just been too difficult, and all this from Tracy just makes it so much worse. I can't stand her or her friends. I'm gutted that I can't play netball and well… Jamie, I miss him."

"I know mate, I don't give a toss about Tracy and her gross mates. I don't care what she thinks or what she tries to get other people to think. I know that it's a nightmare at the moment, but it will get better. You know that you can talk to me if you want to." She looks at me. Her expression is sincere, as it always is. My one constant friend.

"I know, really I do. Let's get to art." We walk as quickly as I can to the art studio.

Just before my bedtime, I write my diary.

Date: April 10th

Horrendous day. BH wrote a note and put on notice board. It said that I love Sky. FFS. ♥ and everything. I think everyone saw it. People were laughing. Saying that we are gay. God, why won't she leave me alone.

My phone pings and I look at the screen. A DM on my Instagram from Sky shows. I open it. "Hi mate, hope you're okay, know today was tough. I don't want to make it any worse, but I was just wondering if you had set up another Instagram account?"

I reply, "No course not, why?"

"There's one that refers to us two, have a look… it's called, *I LOVE SKY."*

Oh my God. "I will have a look; I'll get back to you. CUL8R"

I sign off and then press search on my Instagram account, looking for the one that Sky mentioned. There it was. An Instagram account just full of all of the pictures of me and Sky taken from both of our Facebooks, Instagram's and twitter accounts. Anyone who doesn't know us, would assume that it is detailing our love affair.

"Don't worry Abbie, it doesn't matter, does it. You and Sky have always been friends. You will stay friends now." Jamie's voice couldn't have come at a better time.

I know, I think. It's just unfair that she is allowed to get away with this. I text Sky. "Oh my God, how could she do this? What are we going to do?" I ask.

"I know mate, it's a nightmare. We could just ride it out and not let her know that it has bothered us. What do you think?" Sky is incredulous and clearly annoyed.

"We could, I guess but I really want to make her pay. I just don't know how to do that. Do you have any thoughts? I can't believe it. I want to just get on with stuff without looking out for her next move." I reply.

"Let's talk about it tomorrow, we can work out a plan to sort her out and stop this, what do you reckon? She is horrible and we need to make it work, whatever we do. Night." She signs off.

"Night mate." I respond, not knowing if she is still online and whether she will receive it.

Standing at the bottom of Big Hill, waiting for Sky, I could swear I can hear the laughter and giggles of children in the air. I look around, thinking that there must be a birthday party somewhere, but on a school day, unlikely.

Within minutes of me arriving, Sky shouts me from the road. "Freak head, I'm here." She walks the distance between us and apologises for being a little late, explaining that her mum had been on nights and had only just arrived home after a busy night shift in the accident and emergency unit of St Matthews.

This stops me short. Maybe she saw me and Jamie when we were taken to hospital from the accident? I never asked and Sky never said. Maybe that would be one of those confidential things that she wouldn't be able to tell her family, a little like when dad couldn't talk to us about what he was dealing with and who it concerned.

"No worries," I say, "did you finish your science project and your English revision?"

"Yeah, every night is a party night round at mine!" she says, smiling. "Did you have any thoughts about Tracy and the Instagram account?" It is clearly on her mind, just as it is on mine. I had been thinking about this, but I hadn't come up with anything yet.

"No, you?" I ask.

"No, what do you think we could do?" she pauses and then continues, "We need to find a way to embarrass her, make her feel small. That's all she is trying to do to us."

"Trying and succeeding." I say, "But what would make her feel small? She has more money than I have ever seen. She isn't butt-ugly…"

"If only," Sky agrees. "That would make it so easy."

We carry on the journey to school. Now that I have lost the crutches and my leg is a little stronger, we can venture further up the hill, reducing the distance to the school. The weather is unpredictable, and the flash rainstorms are a nightmare for making the pathways further up the hill impassable. Thankfully, for some reason, maybe global warming? Who knows? The weather has been much better, and the rainy days have been few and far between.

On our arrival at school, it is clear that our time to consider the 'Tracy' problem was going to be limited. We are told in assembly that we are having our mock exams in two weeks' time and so the preparation for exams become the priority for us.

We attend each of our lessons with a renewed energy, wishing we could just absorb the information rather than having to write it all down and remember it. Thankfully, our last lesson is cancelled as our teacher is ill and there wasn't enough time to get a substitute teacher. We all pretended to be disappointed and although we are given the opportunity to revise in the classroom allocated to the lesson we are now missing; we choose to go home.

CHAPTER 8

The Loss of Two Brothers

I arrive home a full hour early, even though me and Sky walk around the bottom of the hill. We needed some extra time to try and conjure a devilish plan to punish Tracy Parsons but this was still not productive and resulted in us just talking about how much she needs teaching a lesson without being able to create a plan to enable us to do this.

When we separated, we promised to contact each other by text and WhatsApp in the evening and we walked to our respective homes.

I walk through the back door as I see Mum's car on the driveway. It has been repaired but it somehow feels different now and I secretly wish that it had been too damaged to repair or that she had sold it. I hate getting in it since that was where Jamie died. There is another car on the road that I don't recognise. A visitor?

I shout to Mum as I entered the kitchen, "I'm home, Mum. Last lesson was cancelled..." I have to stop as I see something that takes my breath away. Luke Harris, the man who drove the car that killed Jamie, is sitting at our kitchen table. He is drinking tea and there is a small plate of biscuits sitting on the table, between him and Mum.

"What the hell?" I say. I am incredulous. "Why are you here?" I did remember what Sky had said and what Gemma had told everyone about their brother dying in the army, but I wasn't told that he was going to be invited. It then dawns on me, I am not supposed to be here, I am supposed to be at school, in geography had the teacher turned up, I would never have known that he had been at the house. What a betrayal. How dare she.

"Hi Abbie, you remember Luke?" Mum asks, stupidly, I think.

"Hi Abbie, I hope you don't mind me being here. I can imagine it's a bit of a shock to see me. I wasn't aware you didn't know I was coming," Luke tells me.

"No, big surprise." I say. "Why are you here?"

"Abbie, please don't be rude," Mum remonstrates with me.

"No, I understand that this is difficult" says Luke, holding his hand up and leaning forward to touch Mums' forearm.

"You understand absolutely nothing! How could you? You will never meet the people who killed your brother. Whereas the person who killed mine is sitting in my kitchen, having tea and biscuits with my mum," I say.

"Fair point," he admits. "But will you hear me out, please?" He looks pleadingly towards me. I look over to Mum and she has a similar expression and nods weakly.

I let my school bag drop on the floor, ignoring the loud crash it makes, and drag out a kitchen chair opposite Luke. "Well?" I say.

"I cannot say I am sorry enough. The day the accident happened was the worse day of my life, and yours I know… Oh God, hang on…" he is flustered. I don't think he thought I would sit down and that he would be given this opportunity to explain. Now he has it, he is not prepared.

"I got a letter that morning, from my brother, he was in Afghanistan, in the army. It had been posted about two weeks before. The letters always take a long time to get home, especially if there are any issues where he is.

He told me he was coming home. I was ecstatic, I can't tell you. But then, only about an hour later, after I got the letter, someone from the army arrived at our front door. I thought it was him to begin with. It wouldn't have been, I know but I was so excited that he was coming home that I couldn't think straight. I ran to the door and threw it open, but it wasn't him. It was a force chaplain and with him was a casualty assistance officer. They asked if they could speak to my brother's next of kin. My mum was in the house and she invited them in. We all knew why they were there, but you almost need to hear them say it, you know?" He looks at us. The room is silent, it is important for us to hear the whole story and I think it is probably important for him to say it. "Well," he continues. "They came in and told us how heroic my brother was…"

I note the past tense and remember me using the past tense for the first time when I was talking about Jamie…

"They told us that he had been killed by an IED when he was on a road check. He was on this deployment with three colleagues and all of them were killed in the explosion, along with the family in the car, carrying the explosives. He had volunteered for the duty as it was the daughter's birthday of the soldier who was supposed to be doing it, but my brother wanted to give him the opportunity to Skype his daughter on her special day. They said how sorry they were for our loss and that the army had bereavement counselling available for the families of serving officers. One of them handed my mum a leaflet and they then picked up their bags and started to the door, talking about more information in a phone call next week where Mum will be told about his body coming back to the UK." Luke takes a breath and looks up for the first time in so long. "As soon as they left, I hugged my mum and we both cried so hard. I was sobbing like a baby. My brother had meant so much to me, he had been my role model, I wanted to be like him, hell, I wanted to be him. I couldn't believe he wasn't going to be here for me, that I wasn't going to see him anymore. Part of me died and I know that Mum felt the same. I felt really sorry for her as well. He was her first child and I had seen her worrying constantly when he was on deployment, waiting for his phone calls and letters, any confirmation that he was okay. I stayed at home, with her for about an hour and then I couldn't stand it. It was so claustrophobic, I couldn't breathe. I needed to get out, to get away from the house. The house that I expected him to return to. I picked up my car keys and got in my car. I know I shouldn't have driven at that time. I can't tell you how sorry I am that I made that decision, but I was going mad where I was. I drove out of our road and onto the main road, but I needed to be further away and decided to go onto the motorway. I wasn't driving too fast, I know I wasn't, but I wasn't concentrating at all. I could just see my brother's face in front of me. I was crying and couldn't see properly. Then I hit your car. I didn't even see it; I couldn't avoid it as I didn't register it was there. I am so sorry. I know that nothing I say will make up for what I have done, but I honestly could not be more angry and upset with myself for the devastation I have caused and I know that I have taken one life but ruined, so many more." He looks exhausted.

Mum is crying, her tear-soaked tissue is useless now and she pulls another from the open box on the table. "Oh Luke, I don't know what to say…" she stands up and walks around the table, her hand dragging on the surface as she maneuverers around the end of the table. When she stands next to Luke, she opens her arms and invites him to hug her. Luke stands up on what look to be very weak legs, tentatively allowing them to take his body weight and collapsing onto my mum. Her arms envelope him in a tight embrace and they both cry with shared grief and the loss of a son and brother for each family.

I feel lost. I needed to feel angry towards Luke but right now, can only feel pity towards him. I can't think of anything to say. I certainly don't want to join in the mutual hugging. I need to be on my own and deal with this. I stand up slowly, trying to minimise the amount of scraping noise from my chair on the tiled floor. My mum opens one of her arms in my direction, inviting me to join them. I shake my head vigorously and pick up my school bag and walk slowly from the room. I don't look back as I walk upstairs to my room.

#

'OMG, you will not believe what she has done now… she only invited Jamie's murderer into our kitchen.' I text Sky. This is slightly unfair, having heard his side of this but somehow I wanted to be angry at him, otherwise all my anger will be directed towards myself for still being alive and Jamie for not.

Sky texts back right away, 'Really, how did that go?' It's so difficult to sense emotion from texts but I want to think that she said it in a shocked and incredulous way, so that's the tone that I use when I read it. Although from our previous conversation, I guess that this interpretation may not be completely accurate.

'He told me about his brother and how he died and how he couldn't see the road when he was driving, didn't see our car! Shouldn't have been driving!' I text back quickly. I can feel my resolve altering when I mention his brother and think about his reaction to the news about his brother's death, how similar it was to mine.

'He lost a brother too. Gemma was right. God, how awful.' I pause before I respond. I am struggling to keep my anger with him. I know that I will never forget what he has done but can I forgive him? I had never considered this before. Mum had mentioned it at the graveyard, but I had dismissed it then. Am I capable of forgiveness, even for this? I am not sure.

"What would you do in that situation? Didn't you just want to be alone, to get away when Mum told you about me?" came a voice in my head. I remembered how desperately I wanted to be on my own, how I couldn't believe that it was true. I was stuck in the hospital with a busted leg but if I wasn't. If I could drive. Would I have done that? Even if it didn't make any sense whatsoever to do that. Even if I would put other people in danger. I don't know but I can't say that I wouldn't.

I decide to leave this discussion and change the subject. I have a lot to process and it would be much easier to do that with Sky, face to face.

"Have you thought about BH? Any ideas what we can do?" I ask on text. We always reduce Tracy Parsons to BH or Bitch-head in our texts, it is shorthand that we both understand.

"No, you?"

"A few but TBH the first thing I think we should do is to ignore the Instagram site. I know it's annoying, her saying stuff about us, but I don't care if people think we're more than friends, what does it matter? Do you think that's a plan?" I ask. I have seen a couple of my friends torn apart socially because they had the courage to 'come out' to their so-called friends, who promptly destroyed them on various chat rooms and platforms. It's horrible and I don't want her to take any satisfaction that she has done this to either one of us.

"Agreed. So, what can we do to quietly let her know we know it's her and that what she is doing has to stop?" she asks. I expected this reaction but am pleased at the same time. Most of the trolling has been directed to me and she could just tell me to ignore it, but this alliance gives me the strength to fight back.

"Let's keep our eyes open for something that's going to hurt her or turn her friends against her, she's nothing on her own." Divide and conquer, my grandad always said to me. He was actually talking about netball practice, but the principle is the same, I think.

"Great idea. Big Hill tomorrow? I'm knackered."

"Yeah, sure. Night." I reply. I see one more reply from her before I wipe my WhatsApp screen.

"Night, Freak head."

CHAPTER 9

Exams and Other Stresses

At school there are posters everywhere and the teachers are constantly reminding us that the end of year exams are in May. That we need to study and how influential the results of these exams will be when it comes to the next year of school. No pressure then…

The year above (fourth year) are doing last-minute prep for first year of their final GCSE exams so their results at this time of year are really important and I have one year to go before this is my concern, thankfully. You can easily pick out those in their final two years. Not only are their ties a different colour but they are the kids with bitten-down fingernails, dark circles under their eyes and very irritable in the corridors, in the playground and canteen queue.

Irrespective of how desperate I am to rejoin the sports teams I used to captain, I think it will take too long to repair the damage caused by the accident. My physiotherapy is going well, and I am now able to jog around the sports hall lightly, but the twisting and turning involved in competitive team games is still beyond me so I spend tiresome evenings after school watching the netball and hockey squads play visiting school teams, wishing I was playing and knowing that I would do better than those currently on the pitch. If only my leg was better.

The abuse from Tracy has waned, probably as a result of the pressure of the exams looming. I know that her parents are expecting her to do well and I heard that they've employed several private tutors to support her in revising all her subjects before each exam date. Her relentless schedule is affecting her mood and albeit she is as aggressive and horrible as ever, she seems to be directing this more to the people immediately around her which included her two closest friends, Amber and Paula, both of whom appear to be getting sick of the constant criticism and berating. They can be seen huddled together, without Tracy, obviously upset with their current treatment. Not surprising really, especially considering just how loyal they had been over the years.

It seems that my plans to separate Tracy from her friends could now be shelved as she is doing that job for us, using her own undeniable skills of empathy and communication, I think, ironically.

During this time, maybe as a 'light at the end of the tunnel,' for all students undergoing the exam regime, we have all been given a letter to take home. This is a letter, addressed to our parents, inviting interest in an outward-bound course in North Wales in June this year. Those selected will be able to take part in rowing, hiking, abseiling, campfires and orienteering.

I had never taken part in any of these activities and really wanted to give them a go. Although my leg is still preventing competitive sports, when I speak to my physiotherapist, she is happy for me to apply for the course, as long as she is able to provide a covering note explaining the limits to my movement and leg strength. "Can't have you coming back injured again, now can we?" she says, as she winks and lays her hand on my shoulder. I am sure she is trying to comfort me.

I assure her that there will be doctors and medically trained staff at the site, and she is relieved and compiles a covering letter for me to submit, along with the application form that my mum has to complete and sign. I had taken the form to the physiotherapist first as, if she said no, my mum would never agree to allowing me to go. It made sense to do it that way round.

I then take the letter home to Mum. Money for school trips is always a problem, we haven't had an actual holiday as a family for years, even before dad died. But I offer to put my meagre birthday and Christmas money to it to help to pay for the place on the course and the £10 spending money we are allowed to take with us.

Some number crunching and promises of good – no, great – behaviour, and she agrees to sign the parental consent form. The instalment option is the saving grace and just because I am aware of this doesn't mean that I discussed the course payment with her. She is still sensitive about our financial situation and I know I am asking a lot, just to go.

Within the consent form, it details the possible disabilities of the applicants and suggests reasonable adjustments. I am unsure what that means but I Google 'reasonable adjustment' and find that it is what's in place to enable those people to go. Strangely I'm in that category. How the mighty have fallen, I can hear Tracy saying, but in a way she's right.

Before the accident, people wanted to *be* me, now people don't even want to be with me, forgetting I exist. Name no longer on the fixture list and never will be again. Who am I?

I tell Sky that I am applying for the outward-bound course, expecting her to say that she is too and begin making plans to sleep next to each other in the dorm, have midnight feasts and sing songs around the campfire, but she looks disappointed. Although she took the form home intending to go, she came back unable to. Her family has already booked a week away in Ibiza during the time of the course, so it's not even a possibility.

So, I will be going, without Sky, and Tracy Parsons will also be there, probably. She has never missed a school trip, whether it has been skiing, trip to Rome for geography course work or London museums for art. Money is not a barrier for her.

"Don't worry Abbie, I'll be there too," Jamie's voice reassures me.

#

The exam time came so quickly, it felt like we had only just got back to school after Easter when we were given our exam timetables and given study leave to do our last-minute preparation. When I received mine, I was shocked about how many exam papers I had in my schedule and how poorly prepared I felt. I compared my timetable with Sky's and as we were doing mostly the same subjects, except for history and sociology. Sky has no interest in the social world, or at least, the current one; preferring to concentrate on the kings and queens of the Tudors, Stuarts and Windsors and the various wars, political decrees and famines in the last five hundred years.

Date: May 6th
First exams are tomorrow. Sociology in the morning and maths in the afternoon. OMG, I have revised for hours and I can't remember anything. WTF am I going to do?

I remember that the first history paper isn't until next week according to Sky's timetable, so I will have to get to school on my own in the morning. My phone pings, indicating a message. I check the phone, it's from Sky, 'Hi freak head, good luck in the morning. See you @ sch after lunch.'

'Thanks weirdo, I can't remember anything. 2 much 2 do,' I reply.

'Don't worry, FH, you'll be fine. See you soon. Sleep well. zzzz' she replies. I don't answer.

I am tired the following morning. I had struggled to sleep due to the stress of the impending exam papers and the pressure to do well, to try and get something positive out of this year. It has seemed like a lost cause but if I do well in my exams, it might give Mum something to be grateful for. I need to prove to myself that I am not useless... In truth, I feel scared.

I set off for school early as I will be walking on my own. I walk around the base of the big hill. There had been rain in the evening before and the thickening grasses underfoot are slippery and difficult to negotiate. As I leave the big hill and mount the pavement adjacent to the road outside the school, I am aware how wet my feet and legs are. There are also blades of green and yellow grasses poking out from my shoes and socks, pricking my feet and ankles.

I walk into school, along with so many nervous looking third years. The fourth and fifth years don't start their exams till next week so all the students taking exams are in my own year. I look around the playground for any friendly faces, but it seems that when there are exams looming concentration is taken away from friendships and becomes a manic delve in the archives of the revision that has been attempted. For me, I am glad I can't see anyone I want to talk to, as I'm not sure that I could hold a coherent conversation anyway.

As I walk into the hall, 'in exam conditions' I see the wet footprints I am leaving behind me and I'm glad my mum can't see them, she'd do her nut.

#

"Put your pens down. The exam is now concluded," Mrs Allen says. We all put our pens down in clatter of plastic against Formica. "Lift your chairs, do not scrape them backwards! Don't forget any of your belongings and you may leave the room row by row. Jason, can you organise the pupils to leave the hall?" She directs this question to a fifth-year prefect, standing at the back of the hall, who immediately puffs out his chest and starts ordering everyone around, very loudly.

"Come on, one row at a time. Listen to me, I'm a prefect." Bless him. It's like Canute holding back the tide. Neither were successful and both were misinformed about the power their position gave them.

As I left the hall, I was pushed into the wall by the leaving crowd. Concerned about damaging my leg, I waited for the majority of people to leave the hall before I attempted the doorway.

When I finally leave the hall, I look through the windows opposite the doors and see Sky in the playground. She had arrived early and appeared to be looking for me. I hurry through the last part of the corridor and leave the building, walking up the four brick steps to the playground.

"Sky!" I shout. She looks over and smiled.

"How did it go?" she asks.

"It was okay. It was tough but I managed to answer most of the questions. The last question was for ten marks. That was hard, my head was fuzzy by then, so I don't think I got much of that." I feel a little despondent but in truth, I had done my best.

We sit and have lunch together and Sky gives me the Twirl that she had bought me. "To keep your strength up," she says, and within minutes we are called back into the hall to sit our maths exam.

To say that the maths exam is difficult would be an understatement. I don't find maths easy at the best of times but under these conditions, I can't even count the fingers on the hand in front of me. When are we ever going to need the mean and mode of anything, or be able to work out quadratic equations or know how long it takes a bus to travel to Cardiff, driving at sixty miles an hour, with twelve passengers, all weighing an average of thirteen stones each in moderate traffic, with two tea stops? I ask you. Pointless in my opinion.

Exhausted, we both leave the exam hall and make our way to the school exit. Everyone walking with us looks shell-shocked and miserable. At least it isn't just me. Sky looks a little more confident, but she has always been better than me at maths, so that is to be expected.

It is a relatively silent journey home. I say relatively because, as we walk around the bottom of the big hill, I could swear that I can hear children laughing again. Another party? No, surely not. I look around but can't see any groups of children who might be making the sounds. I stop to see if I am able to pinpoint where the laughter is coming from. Sky continues to walk on at first but then recognises that I'm not with her and turns around.

"Freak Head, you ok?" she asks. She attempts to follow my gaze but there is nothing to see and she stands perplexed. "Freak Head?"

"Can't you hear the kids laughing?" I ask, still looking around, but I realise that I can only hear the sound when the wind is coming down the hill towards me.

"No, I can't, I don't know what you are listening to, but I can only hear the cars and the wind in the trees, over there." She points over to the left of us, where there is an old copse of trees.

"Yes, you're probably right," I say, unconvinced.

We separate and plan to text after we had both had dinner, if there is time, as we both have science revision to do tonight for tomorrows exams.

As I continue my journey home, I think about the kids voices I heard. They sounded quite young. Their voices appeared to travel on the air. On the air? What the hell am I thinking? Am I going mad? The exams, lack of sleep. Missing Jamie? Maybe that's why I hear him, because I'm stressed and miss him?

I have a restless night and wake to an empty house. Mum has gone out, she hasn't said where, but it must be important. I text to ask her but receive no reply. I input her details on 'find friends' and it takes a while to register her location, but when it does, I see that she is at Costa in the High Street. Intrigued and a little worried, I ring her. The call goes straight to voicemail, I speak quietly, trying not to sound concerned, "Hi Mum, I guess you couldn't sleep either. If you get this message, can you ring me to let me know you're okay? I'm going to school soon, got science…" the phone makes a long beeping sound and I know that I have reached the capacity of the message allowance. I don't receive her response prior to leaving for the big hill. When I get there, unusually, Sky is waiting for me.

"Yo, Freak head!" She shouts, when I am a few metres away. I wave, smiling. I am not sure where the nickname came from, but I don't mind it at all. I actually can't remember a time when we didn't use the name between us.

#

When I get home after school, Mum is sitting in the kitchen drinking coffee.

"You alright, Mum?" I ask. I think it's best not to jump right in with questions about where she was this morning. I am really curious, but I don't want her to think that I don't trust her.

"Yeah, sweetie. How did your exams go? Do you think you did okay?" she asks.

"As well as I could, I guess." I reply. I leave a pause and she fills it, thankfully.

"Sorry I wasn't here when you left. I know you would have been worried, but I had to go somewhere. I wanted to wish you good luck, but I had to go somewhere." She looks regretful and is pulling a piece of kitchen roll apart on her lap.

"Where were you, Mum? Is there anything wrong. I thought you had left me. I was on my own." I hadn't realised that I felt that way, the words come out and I can't stop them. As I watch my mum's reaction to what I am saying, it is clear that my words are like weapons to her. This wasn't my intention, but I am suddenly feeling really vulnerable. What if she had been hurt? I couldn't contact her, didn't know where she was.

"I am really sorry, I should have left a note, I was hoping to get back before you left. I am so sorry." She pauses, she is breathing hard and can't catch my eye. "I don't want you to be upset, but I got a call this morning from Luke, he was desperate, crying on the phone. He said he was going to go to the train station to end it all, he felt so guilty about what happened to you and Jamie. I had to go and try and stop him." She is in tears.

"What happened, did you stop him?" I ask, concerned for both my mum but also for Luke.

"Yes, thankfully but it took a long time to talk him down. He was so upset. I really didn't know if I was going to be able to do it. He is so messed up about the accident, Abbie. I feel so sorry for him."

"What's he going to do? Why did he call you? Don't you think it's a bit weird that he called you?" I ask.

"I thought you might say that, but he told me that his mum is a mess, she can't help him and he feels bad that he can't help her to deal with how she feels at the moment. He knows that if anything happens to him, she will be in a worse position, but he can't help how he feels. He is really struggling. His life has fallen apart." She pauses, looking away. This is clearly affecting her.

I walk over to her and put my arm around her. She immediately stands and holds me so tightly. Her reaction is so quick and unexpected, it takes me by surprise. I realise that we haven't really hugged like this since the accident. I know I have been distant, not that I wanted to be, but it has been hard to open-up to anyone. I can understand my mum's reaction to Luke's phone call.

that's her character, she has always been the caretaker and she probably need someone to 'replace' Jamie, someone to need her. I know I have not wanted her to coddle me. Maybe if I had she wouldn't have been as keen to speak to him, who knows?

CHAPTER 10

Not So Grand

The rest of our exams continue for the following two weeks with varying degrees of satisfaction and disappointment at my own ability to answer the questions posed. Although I won't know the results until just before we leave school for summer, which will be around 19th July, so long to wait.

There is one saving grace during this time, as all the school netball games have been suspended because the schools in our league are also in their exam time and they don't want to distract the players and put them at a disadvantage. They will pick up again straight after the exams have finished, with our first match being against Wauluds Bank High School: a school renowned for expert players who seem to have boundless energy. I remember playing them when I was captain and centre. It was always a tough match. They were clean, but they were good.

Even though I try to stay away from the netball games right now, I think I will watch this one. It will be a good test for the new captain, and I would be interested to see what Zoe does to manage it. I could give her some tips, but I don't think she would appreciate the coaching and I don't really feel inclined to offer.

The following week and the exams are complete, and we can all breathe a sigh of relief. I agree with Sky to meet her after school. We stand on the edge of the netball pitch waiting for the two teams of players to come out of the respective changing rooms. I can picture what is going on in there. Zoe will be speaking to the players trying to give them a pep talk, a difficult thing ordinarily but even worse considering that they have lost their last four matches. It's hard to know how she is going to motivate them in view of this. The other captain will undoubtedly be aware of our current league position and will be more confident about their chances against us.

It's quite clear that my estimation of the locker room captains briefing is accurate as the visiting team come out of the changing rooms bouncing around, throwing the balls to each other and are noisy to the extreme. Our team is already beaten. They walk out of the school, hands in tracksuit top pockets, hardly talking and not looking above eyeline. It is a shame that they have to play to the end of time, it would be less embarrassing to forfeit the game rather than suffer the defeat that they endure.

As we are talking about when we should leave, there is a familiar voice from behind us, "The lovebirds are out on a date, are they?" Tracy laughs. Amber and Paula giggle from beside her. "Don't like the look of yours, Sky, scraping the barrel for this one, weren't you?"

"Piss off why don't you!" I whisper.

"Don't you wish you hadn't come? Such a Jonah! Bad luck wherever you go." Tracy continues maliciously as she walks around to the opposite side of the pitch.

I'm fuming. I decide to leave so I walk out of the school grounds with Sky about ten minutes before the end. The visiting team from Wauluds Bank are already unreachable and it feels cruel to watch the death throes on the pitch from our team.

We walk across the road outside the school and through the broken stone wall to the trees surrounding

Big Hill, all the way talking about Tracy and calling her such terrible names. Our joint dislike of Tracy reinforces our solidarity. Walking through the trees in dusk is spooky. Cracking twigs under our feet seems much louder than they do in the daylight. Although it isn't dark yet, it might as well be. We hold on to each other to prevent us from tripping but also because both of us are a little scared, although neither of us admit this. It is quite a thin copse of trees, which then leads to the big hill. As the light grows at the edge of the tree line, we begin to quicken our pace, making the uneven ground more dangerous as we aren't really paying attention to where we are walking, paying more attention to where we want to be.

It is a relief to be in the open air. The trees seem oppressive and I vow not to return to them in the dark, under any circumstances. As we get on to the hill, Sky says, "Race you to the grand house." She starts running up the hill. "Come on Freak head!"

"Sky, I can't run," I start jogging up the hill, not hoping to catch up to Sky. "Slow down…" Sky stops at the stone steps at the centre of the front of the house. The mansion is falling in places and would not be livable by today's standards, but it was once beautiful. There are three floors. The two front doors with huge brass knobs in the centre of each of the doors, each doorknob as big as one of my hands, both still in place. To either side of the front doors are two tall windows and five windows on both the second and third floors, making it appear symmetrical in design. There is hardly any roof but what is left shows that the roof was massive and probably hid an expansive loft space, which might have been servants' quarters at some point. The remaining roof is covered in old red clay tiles and there were some tiles on the ground around the building, maybe blown off in high winds over the years or bombed in the war. If Luton was bombed. I feel I should know if my town was bombed, but I don't.

Around the building itself is a stone patio with stone railings circling the remaining structure and pillars at either side of the front doors, holding two massive stone plant pots, like ceramic urns. There are weeds sticking out of the top of the pots, nothing healthy, just ghostly twigs really.

I have never seen this place up close and its only being so close that I can imagine all the fine teas and dinners that may have taken place here centuries ago. Sky walks over to the window at the left of the front door and peers in.

"What's it like? Sky, what can you see?" I ask. I start walking towards her, climbing the stone stairs adjacent to the door.

"Come and see," She says, waving her hand to me, indicating to me to walk towards her. "Look, can you see the dining table, it's still set for… one, two, three, four…" she continued counting the place settings, tracing the table settings with her finger on the filthy window, "eleven, twelve."

"I wonder who the last people who ate here were? Do you think it was people from the war? Wasn't it a hospital for service men?" I ask, slightly embarrassed about my lack of local knowledge.

"It was, but that's not the last time it was used. I thought it was an institution, like a mental hospital in the fifties and sixties, but why would they set the table? Would they set a table? I guess they have to eat, but would they have knives on the table with the criminally insane at dinner?" Sky is think-talking, she does it a lot. I always find it funny, but she says she doesn't know she's doing it. She runs through her thoughts out loud so I can hear her but when I tell her that she is doing it, it always comes as a shock to her.

"How do you know that they were criminally insane? Maybe there were just a little mad rather than criminal. It's close to the public, what would happen if they escaped? Everyone would be in danger, wouldn't they? There are no bars on the windows, so nothing to keep them here," I reason.

"But this was years ago, loads of these houses are newer than that. So, there might not have been public in the area. Maybe they were criminally insane. Maybe they killed each other. Do you think that anyone died here? It feels spooky, like there are secrets here. Can you feel it?" she asks. She is crossing her arms and rubbing the tops of her arms as a chill appears to have run down them.

"It does feel eerie, like things have happened here, but it doesn't feel sinister to me. I don't feel scared, not really. It's weird. Shall we go?" I ask. I am intrigued by the house and decide to look it up on the internet when I get home.

"Okay," says Sky. She follows me as I make my way down the hill. The long grasses wrap around our ankles, causing us to stop and pull our feet out of tangled grasses many times on the way. We are laughing all the way down the hill. It is nice to feel normal for the first time in such a long time. The air is a little cooler, although that didn't really explain the chill at the back of my neck. Instinctively, I raise my hand and cover my neck with my hand and turn around to see if there is anyone behind us. Sky carries on, oblivious to my discomfort, she has overtaken me as grasses claim my foot and I have, yet again, to pull it backwards, out of the divot of twisted blades. Having stopped anyway, I turn around, at which point I see the shadows of people disappearing into the grand house. I strain to see but I can't see anything more and decide that it was probably a trick of the light. It is dusk and I have obviously seen shadows cast by the trees, moving in the wind and my imagination was probably fuelled by the conversation we had outside the house.

"Come on, Freak head!" Sky is at the bottom of the hill. I turn towards her and in that second, decide not to tell her about what I had seen. I don't know why I have made that decision, but it feels right.

"Sorry, got my foot caught," I shout to her, as I make my way down towards her.

"Idiot!" she says, when I reach her, laughing.

I bump into her saying, "Whoa!" We both fall over. When we get up, we continue to walk home, giggling.

"See you tomorrow, Freak head" Sky says as the road separates and she walks towards her house.

"Text after dinner, I'll be in my room," I say.

"You know it," She says. I hear her laughing as she disappears around the bend in her road.

Date: 31st May

A busy couple of weeks. Luke Harris phoned Mum, was gonna top himself and she went to see him. She stopped him. I'm glad she did but she might care about him more than she cares about me. I must try and be nicer to her. How would I feel if my son died? Especially if he was only nine years old. But she doesn't seem to know that I am struggling too. I really need to talk to someone, but she doesn't want to talk to me about Jamie. It helps that I can still talk to him, it's like he is still here. Still with me.

The netball team is not doing well. I shouldn't be glad, and it is really bitchy to be glad, I know but I don't want them to do too well without me. I want them to regret that I am not there. I don't feel that I matter to them. Went to the last game and it was a nightmare. We lost AGAIN! Zoe is not a good captain, a bad choice.

BH was there and pushed into me and Sky. COW! She isn't right in the head. She said we were on a date night! I wish she would pick on someone else, leave us alone.

Went to the grand house. Its gorg inside. It doesn't feel evil there. Didn't see the white lady but saw some people going into the house when we were nearly down the hill – didn't tell Sky. Not told her about hearing Jamie either, seeing things and hearing voices, she might think I'm going mad.

Exams were rubbish, especially science, maths and sociology.

Going to the outward-bound course next week. Can't wait. Can't believe Sky can't go. Going shopping over the weekend to get my stuff for the trip.

I sign off the diary entry, I'm happy to write this amount of detail, as Dave has never asked to read my journal.

CHAPTER 11

Bittersweet Goodbye

My mum and I tramp the streets of Luton town centre and the mall to try and find everything on the resources and clothing lists provided by the outward-bound course organisers. I know that we can't afford to get the same gear as some of my classmates, but if I am able to stay warm and dry, I will be fine. All our food and drinks are provided by the programme leaders and we can hire specialist equipment at the site at a reduced cost, which pleases Mum as ropes, harnesses and helmets would stretch our budget far too far.

By Saturday afternoon, we have ticked everything off the list. Mum has even treated me to a new set of pyjamas as I had mentioned my concern of wearing my old set. I couldn't imagine putting them on in front of Tracy Parsons with all their frayed edges and the hole on the left elbow. It's going to be bad enough being there whilst she is showing off her designer clothes and equipment.

'Got all my stuff for Wales,' I text Sky, when I get home.

'Brilliant, what colour is your bikini?' she texts back with a smiley emoji.

'Weirdo!' I text. 'When do you go to Ibiza?' I ask.

'Tomorrow, Mum's frantic. She has repacked four times. We have weighed the cases on the bathroom scales to make sure they're under but one's still a bit heavy. How much stuff have you got to take?' she asks.

'I've got a fair bit but got it all in my rucksack.'

'Is BH going?' she asks, she knows that I am worried about Tracy coming and me not having her to support me.

'Yeah, think so.' I input a sad emoji. 'She is going to make my life a misery. Do you know if Amber or Paula are going?' I ask. I don't know why but I think that Tracy might be less of a threat if she is on her own. I remember when Amber and Paula had been talking about Tracy behind her back, when she was picking on them during the exam revision classes.

'No, I saw the list of the people going, they weren't on it. Tracy definitely was though,' she says. I feel immediately reassured. Although I will have to deal with Tracy at least she will not be flanked by the other two, who seem to provide her strength that she doesn't possess on her own.

'I wonder how princess Tracy will cope sleeping in a tent, without three meals a day and having to fend for herself?' I text. It has just occurred to me that I am not going to be the one disadvantaged whilst we are away. I have had very little and been able to cope. Tracy has never had to.

'OMG. Didn't think of that. You're right. Take lots of pictures, we can have a laugh when we both get back. I wish I was coming with you.' Sad emoji. I'm not sure how truthful this is, I would certainly prefer to go to Ibiza instead of a cold, probably wet hillside in Wales, no matter how pretty it is, and I am sure Sky does too, but it makes me happy that she said it.

'Have a great time, I'll text if I can. Don't know what the Wi-Fi is going to be like. See you when we both get back anyway. xx' I text.

'Bye Freak head,' Sky replies. I put my phone in my jeans back pocket and gather my Wales stuff, placing it all in the corner of the living room. I check the list to make sure that everything was ticked off. I have done this a number of times but feel that I need to do it again to make sure I haven't forgotten it. I am nervous, I will be on my own, without Sky. My mum will be totally on her own for the first time since the accident. I feel very vulnerable at the moment. Only two days before I go.

That night, I disappear into dreams and fitful sleep. "Warm, Abbie, come and find me!" Jamie is hiding in a wood. I can hear his voice, it is clear. He is close. I run in all directions, trying to find him. I need to find him. This feels like so much more than the normal hide and seek he loves.

"Where are you, Jamie? Please help me find you." I can hear my voice, pleading with him. I run left, over the fallen trunks of trees, treading on branches and twigs as I run, slipping on moss gathered on sod mounds around the trunks of the largest trees. Peeking around the wide oaks, hoping to see his little head, his blonde hair tussled by the wind, holding on to the deep cut bark to stop myself from falling.

'Warm, Abbie," he repeats. "Can't you find me? Do you want me to come out?" Jamie sounds disappointed. "Have you given up?"

I can feel my heart beating out of my chest. I want to see him. I need to see him. "Please Jamie, I want to see you," I say.

"But Abbie, if you see me, I will have to go, forever. I am not allowed to talk to you again. It's a rule." He is crying, "I miss you, Abbie, don't make me come out yet.

Please don't give up," he says, imploring me to change my mind.

"Okay, you win. Well done, Jamie. You did well. I can't find you. A great hiding place. I am so proud of you. Please carry on talking to me. I miss you. I don't want to lose you," I say.

"Thank you, Abbie. I love you," Jamie's reply sounds relieved and I immediately relax.

As I open my eyes, it is dark all around me. I am pleased I am in my own bed and am comforted by that. Instinctively, I look around my room for any sign of Jamie. Although I know I won't see him, I cannot help looking, hoping that he might just be there. My head is damp, I am sweating, and my breaths are coming quickly. I feel like I have been running and not just running, but running for my life. I don't remember that part of my dream. I check my phone, which sits on my bedside set of drawers where it is charged nightly and acts as my alarm clock. It is 03:20. I need to sleep. I turn over, away from the window to ensure that the rising sun won't wake me, pulling the blankets to my waist, allowing my body to cool down.

I decide not to speak to Mum about this dream. It wasn't the first time I've had it and, as I am leaving tomorrow, I don't want her to be worried about me. I have still not told her that I am hearing Jamie and, for the moment, I think that its best I keep this to myself.

#

The day before the Wales trip is a tense one at home. The trip is hardly mentioned and Mum seems to be trying to busy herself with all sorts of menial jobs around the house to avoid a conversation which may allude to the prospect of her being on her own for a week and me, her only family, being miles away and out of her protection.

I get my travelling clothes ready so I am not searching for clothes in the morning that I can wear for the journey. My favourite jumper and jeans, my PE pumps and my new weatherproof jacket, bought from the mall, during our shopping trip the day before.

At nine o'clock in the evening I tell Mum that I am going to bed. My disturbed night last night and the nervousness I feel about tomorrow has made me so tired that I need to sleep.

"Okay sweetie, have a good sleep, have you got a glass of water?" she asks.

"Yes, Mum." I mount the stairs with my water and my phone. Having showered and changed into my old pyjamas, I get into bed, pulling my bedclothes up to my chin. I set my alarm and plug it in to the charger, making a mental note to take my charger to my rucksack in the morning, as I will need it whilst I am away.

"Good night, Abbie." I hear Jamie. He is fainter than last night, like he is further away.

"Good night, Jamie." I roll over and close my eyes. Blissful sleep takes me, and I disappear into the twilight world, with fields of grass, hills and small children's laughter surrounding me. I feel happy as I sleep. Relaxed and safe.

The morning of the trip is fraught and difficult. I want to be excited about going but it is hard to feel like that with Mum moping around, telling me that the weather is always bad in Wales, that they speak a different language and I might not understand them, and their food might be inedible. Why can't she just be happy for me? She has spent a fortune on this trip, and she seems to be trying to turn me against going. Is she trying to keep me home? Maybe, I just need to be away, some time for me. If she had let me talk about Jamie, even asked me how I was doing, I might have told her how I am feeling.

"Come on, Abbie." Mum shouts to me at ten in the morning. "We have to be at school at ten thirty. Are you ready to go?" she continues. She sounds slightly despondent.

I gather everything together and make a final check of my rucksack. I pick it up and pull the strap over my right arm, walking out of my bedroom and down the stairs. I reach the bottom and remember my charger. "Wait a minute Mum, forgot my charger." I pull the plug from my wall and wrap the lead around my hand. As I turn around to walk out of the door, I see Jamie's face: a photograph that I forgot I had, sitting slightly behind a book on the shelf near my bedroom door. Much happier times. He is smiling, holding Roger in one hand and an ice cream in the other. It's a warmer day in the photo, and the sun is melting the ice cream he holds, the white liquid running down his hand and on his wrist. Tears run down my face, I don't even realise that I am crying.

"Abbie, come on!" Mum shouts from downstairs.

"Coming, Mum!" I put the picture under my jumper, I don't know how Mum would feel if she knew that I was taking it, although I don't know if she even knew that it was there either.

We leave the house and make our way to the school; it is a warm day and we had lots of time, so we decide to walk. As we turn from the main road and walk up the school drive, I see a few of my school friends arriving with their parents, most of them, like us, have chosen to arrive on foot. One of those coming with us who isn't on foot is Tracy Parsons, who has been driven in by her parents in their brand-new silver BMW. I haven't even been in a BMW.

As she gets out of her parents' car, Tracy pulls a large hold-all from the back seat and puts in on the gravel path next to her car, then reaches back into the car and drags out a NIKE rucksack which she then pushes her arms through and carries on her back. The hold-all is on wheels, which she then lifts by one side and manoeuvres behind her as she joins the rest of us near the school entrance.

Tracy's mum parks her car in the deputy head teacher's parking bay and she and Tracy's dad get out of the car and walk over to Tracy. Who does she think she is? She is definitely not the deputy head, that is Mrs Smith. Why do people like her feel that they have the right to assume that whatever they do is okay? No wonder Tracy is such a bitch. Like mother, like daughter.

The noise is growing amongst the kids and their parents, with some of the girls joining in their usual cliques, excitedly talking about the trip, what they are going to do and how much fun they are going to have.

I stay with Mum. She is struggling, it's obvious.

"She'll be okay, Abbie," Jamie tells me. I close my eyes and try to relax. Opening them, I look at Mum, she looks like a shadow of the person I knew before the accident. She used to be tough and strong, funny and kind, now she is empty and childlike. I feel like I need to look after her. It must be obvious if my nine-year-old spirit brother offers to look after her in my absence.

"You okay, Mum?" I ask quietly, so no one else can hear.

"Of course, sweetie, just remember to call me if you need anything," she says. She finds my hand and squeezes it.

Even though I know that if I contact her with any worries or issues, she will be helpless to do anything about them – she can't even look after herself – I say, "I know Mum, thanks."

At a quarter-to eleven, the coach finally arrives. All the kids go crazy when it comes up the drive and stops in front of us, everyone is so excited.

There is chaos as we all get on the coach, our cases are taken by the driver and loaded in the cargo hold under the seating area, between the coach wheels. By the time the driver has finished with his luggage block building, the hold looks like a version of Jenga or Minecraft – a pang of sadness as I remember Jamie and the hours he spent building the various constructions, plants and recently angular cows in the fields, in his favourite Minecraft game.

I walk up the steps of the bus and turn right towards the tastelessly patterned seats, I walk down the aisle in the centre, separating the pair of seats on either side. I find a seat near to the window adjacent to where my mum is standing, on the path outside the school. I look at her from inside the coach. She looks sad. Looking down, she is wringing her hands, uncomfortable. A bag hits my right shoulder, causing me to jump and look around. I instinctively grab my shoulder with my left hand and lean around to see Tracy walking up the aisle to the back of the bus, laughing and talking loudly to a girl already sitting there.

As the bus engine fires, and a scream rings out from the kids around me. I look out of the window and see mum's head jump up, as if she has only just realised that I am leaving. She smiles at me, but her smile doesn't reach her eyes. I wave at her and mouth soundlessly, "I love you, Mum." She is crying, she waves half-heartedly.

"Love you too," she mouths and then looks away.

CHAPTER 12

An Uncomfortable Coupling

The coach moves forward, and we are off. I look back and Mum has already started to walk down the drive. I don't see her look back.

Mr Comrie, a history teacher, is one of the teachers who is taking us on the coach, he stands at the front, near the driver and shouts, "LISTEN!" This has absolutely no effect on the noise levels. "LISTEN! STOP WHAT YOU ARE DOING OR WE WILL NOT BE GOING TO WALES!" Finally, the kids calm down slightly.

"Thank you." He looked relieved. "We are going to be travelling for about three and a half hours, depending on traffic. If you feel poorly, you need to let one of us know. We will be stopping during the journey, so you can use the toilet. If you have any sandwiches with you, you can eat them on the coach, but you need to make sure you take all of your rubbish off the coach. Has anyone got any questions?" He smiles a pained smile, turns around and sits back down.

As no one sits next to me, I am able to put my lunch beside me and then put my earphones in and start listening to the music on my Spotify playlist. I had made my own lunch, so I knew what I had: tuna and mayo roll, McCoy's salt and vinegar crisps and a Twirl bar, lovely.

Looking out of the window, I watch the roads become wider and busier as we enter the M1. I lean back into the seat, which feels so comfortable, and I am unaware, but my eyes start to close. I drift off into sleep. "Come on, Abbie, you can't find me" Jamie is laughing, breathless. He has been running through the wood, excited, since I said that I would play with him. Who wouldn't? He is so cute when he laughs, and truthfully, he is rubbish at hide and seek. I run over the fence to the wood. I had given him a head start so he is already looking for a decent hiding space before I reach the trees. I see the movement of low hanging branches a little way in front of me. On closer inspection, the small blonde head I recognise so well inches from behind a wide oak tree. Pitiful, I think.

"If only I knew where Jamie was," I say loudly, walking in the opposite direction to where I know he is. There is another person in the wood. I only see a glimpse of them, a woman, in grey. She walks away through the trees and seems to be walking behind the tree that I think Jamie is behind. As she appears at the other side of the tree, her right hand seems to linger behind her, as if she has been holding his hand and has reluctantly let it go. As I watch her through the trees, I am captivated and can't seem to turn away. Irrespective of this, I somehow lose sight of her. She appears to fade into the ether.

I decide to look for Jamie and search behind all the trees and cannot find him. I panic. "Jamie!" I shout. I am struggling to breathe, where is he?

The coach hits a bump in the road throwing me into the window. I bang my head and wake immediately. Sweat is along my hairline and I suddenly feel really alone. I wonder if I have shouted out in my dream and am reassured that no one seems to be paying me any attention, and I know that they definitely would if they had heard me.

The sign for the M6 is overhead and I see Mr Comrie stand again. "EVERYONE!" he shouts. "WE WILL BE STOPPING IN ABOUT TEN MINUTES. WHEN THE COACH STOPS, IF YOU NEED TO GO TO THE

TOILET, YOU NEED TO GO STRAIGHT THROUGH THE CARPARK, WITH MRS ALLEN. YOU MUST COME STRAIGHT BACK TO THE COACH. NO DEVIATIONS!"

The coach continues and then pulls into the services. Having parked at the coach park, those needing to go to the toilet leave the coach. I stay where I am, I hadn't brought a drink with me and didn't need to go.

As we travelled up the M6 and on to the A5, to North Wales, the scenery changes from a mainly flat, slightly industrial landscape to a lush green view with hills becoming taller as we continue. In all, the journey is boring and uneventful. The dream has disturbed me but only because I couldn't find Jamie at the end.

We arrive at the centre at about two-thirty. The driveway is pressed gravel and makes a noisy alternative to the tarmacked motorways that I have become used to. The grey stone buildings resemble those I've seen in the towns we had driven through since leaving the main road, it must be a local stone.

The coach pulls up and we are all invited to alight and reclaim our cases by Mr Comrie. I get up, replace my phone in my pocket and pick up my rubbish, taking it outside and putting it in the bin adjacent to the coach park. I walk around to the luggage area and pick up my large rucksack, slinging it on my back.

"Watch it! You nearly knocked my head off!" shouted a familiar voice behind me.

"Sorry," I said. "Didn't see you." I turned around and saw Tracy, standing too far away to be hit by my bag, but close enough to make a fuss about it.

"Yeah right, whatever!" she says, looking at me as if I was something that she had trod in. I walk away.

"EVERYONE!" It appears that Mr Comrie has become too used to hearing himself shout as he seemed to choose that volume automatically. Irrespective, the lack of coach and road noise has appeared to accentuate his normal voice, and everyone turns around, probably shocked rather than doing as they were told.

"I would like to introduce you to your course leaders. You will be split up into four groups, each will have a leader. This group will be your family for this course, and we will be working on a scoring system, so yes, there will be a competitive element to this week. You need to work as a team within your groups and try to achieve as many points as you can. Points will be awarded for bravery, innovation, teamwork, skills and your ability to complete the various tasks and activities set. Points will be removed for bad behaviour, rudeness and I must remind you that the normal school rules apply whilst we are here. We have been wracking our brains to decide on team names and have decided to call the teams: Metis – titan goddess of wisdom; Kratos – a god of strength and power; Hades – god of the dead, king of the underworld, and Apollo – god of the sun, music, healing, and herding."

There was some chatter as the names for the teams are announced, the kids are seemingly getting themselves into their own groups, probably hoping that if they made a good job of this, the teachers would abandon their own prepared lists.

"Leading Metis will be Jason," Mr Comrie points over to his left. A man in his early twenties stands up and waved. He is slim but muscular, probably the constant training they do. He remains standing.

"In charge of Kratos, is Olivia," he points to a woman on Jason's right. Olivia is a tall, slim woman in shorts and a tee shirt. Her hair is short, and her sunglasses hang around her neck on a fluorescent green cord. "KRATOS!" she shouts.

Mr Comrie smiles and carries on, "Apollo's leader will be Matthew," he points to his left.

"Matt," says a young man, who stands immediately. "Only my mum calls me Matthew, when I'm in trouble." He laughs and then moves to stand with the other leaders.

"And last but not least, for Hades, we have John." The oldest one of the leaders stands. John is a man in his thirties, his face looks a little weathered and he seems to like denim as his shorts and waistcoat are both faded jean material; even his flip flops are frayed denim.

John moves to the leader's group and as he does so, he is handed a piece of paper from Mr Comrie. "Thanks. Dick" the kids laugh loudly. None of us knew his first name, the teachers didn't ever tell us, we have to call them Mr Whatever, Mrs Whoever or Miss Whatsit and the revelation that he had a nickname and that it was a rude word was too much!

John giggles as he realises what he has done. "Settle down, we need to assign your teams…" The crowd gathers themselves and calms down, excited who they will be spending the next six days with and who will be their mortal enemies.

"When I call your name, stand with the leader I assign you to. There will be no discussion or negotiation. You have been assigned your groups and even if you don't like it, you will have to live with it and make it work for you." He looks serious; he is obviously anticipating some disagreement in the fixture lists.

"Behind me, Amanda, Michelle, Richard, David and Rebecca. With Jason, there will be Tracy, Tina, Ronan, Abbie and Latifa. Those with Olivia will be Morgan, Erol, Priti, Jessica and Andrew. Hannah, Susan, Jade, Mohammed and Rhishi will be with Matt." There is a lot of pushing and shoving as the teams are formed. Some are quite happy with their affiliations, I am not. I was hoping that even though I knew that Tracy was coming to the course, that I would be able to keep a safe distance from her and I would not have ever chosen to be on the same team as her. Looking at her face, she feels the same. I wish I hadn't come.

"Stay out of my face, loser," Tracy whispers menacingly close to my ear, as the crowd pushes us together as people bustle past.

I try to stand closer to Jason, to feel safer.

John continues, "Let me run through a bit of an itinerary for the week. We will all be doing all of these activities but some of them have maximum participants so you will do them in your teams. Now I can see from some of your faces that these team choices might not have reflected your own, but you WILL have to work as teams, so you better get used to that and mend your differences. It's that simple." He looks around and there is a matter of fact look about him.

It is NOT that simple, I think. Tracy hates me, I have never known why, and I don't like her. Granted she hasn't got her two henchmen with her but even on her own she's a bit scary.

"Through this week, you may face your worst fears… Have strength and courage to deal with them. Lean on your teammates, they will help you."

I bet she won't, I think.

He continues, "For the rest of today we will be sorting out all of your kit and preparing for the week. Those of you with your own kit can wait in the mess hall, which is where we will all have our meals when we are at the centre, and the rest of us will go to the storerooms. Follow me." He motions to a large building to the left of the coach park. It has similar grey stone bricks and wide garage-like doors, probably for the storage of large equipment, like canoes and kayaks.

Around ninety percent of the kids follow him to the building, and he leads us in. I am grateful that I am in the majority and not one of the few without the funds to spend on equipment, singled out for being poor. That would have been a gift for Tracy.

We are given all our tents, sleeping bags, wet suits, ropes, maps and compasses, along with other smaller pieces, including metal cups, plates and cutlery. John then takes us to the mess hall, and we put our stuff in piles at the side of the canteen area. It is noisy with all the clattering cups and metal poles hitting the floor at once. We are directed to sit in our teams, on separate tables. I find Tina, Tracy and Latifa on a table at the back of the room and sit there, whilst we wait for Ronan to join us.

"Sorry," he says, "needed a waz, long journey." Ronan says, as he sits down.

"Okay, you should all have everything that was on the list that we sent you. If you find that you have forgotten anything or lost anything, please let us know straight away. For those of you renting the equipment, bear in mind that we need everything back, if you lose anything, unfortunately, we will have to send you home with a bill for your parents, so look after everything you have."

There is some chatter around the room… it starts to quieten down as John speaks again.

"Tomorrow, we will be doing some difficult challenge activities and, as we will be sleeping in the woods on Wednesday, we will talk to you about the skills you will need to manage your tents, feeding yourselves and keeping yourselves safe whilst you are outdoors." The fact that we will be sleeping outdoors seems to excite some. Unbelievable. What did they think the sleeping bags and tents were for?

"On Wednesday, during the day, you will be split into your teams and will be able to do a range of activities. There will be rock climbing, hiking and tent-making and self-survival. There will be no individual scores on this day and teamwork will be marked only. The following day will be our wet day with some open water challenges. We will be canoeing, kayaking, rafting, again working in your teams will be essential." There is some chatter around the room. As I can swim, I assume everyone can, but maybe not.

John continues, seemingly oblivious to the hubbub around the room. "We will bring all of the skills that you have learned over the first few days together on the Friday when we will go hiking over the hills surrounding us, testing your map-reading and navigation skills. You will need to find your way, as a team, to a cabin in the centre of the woods at the foot of the mountains and you will be responsible for your own dinner, so I hope there is someone in your team who can cook." We look at each other. Looking at the mystified faces amongst my team members, I doubt it. I am not sure that I would eat a meal prepared by Tracy anyway.

"You will stay in the cabin overnight and make your way back to the centre for breakfast on Saturday." He took a deep breath. It is obvious that he has said all this several times before, but it looked like he wanted to say it all before he forgot it or lost his place in the instructions.

"When you get back and after you have returned all your equipment, we will give you all your scores for the week and present the winning certificates for the team in first place. I have been told by your teachers that when you leave the centre, you will be taken to the local villages so that you can spend any money you have brought for souvenirs or postcards or whatever."

The mess hall erupts in noise when John finishes explaining what we are doing for the week. The other teams seem more inclined to gel and are leaning across the tables they are sitting at, to try and hear each other over the rest of the commotion in the room. Our team is going to struggle, as two of the five members find it hard to be in the same room.

CHAPTER 13

Sharing is Not Always Caring

I look around the room for Jason, he is stood with the other leaders and teachers at the front of the canteen. They are talking and at the end of their conversation, John hands the leaders a piece of paper each and they separate to their relevant tables to join their teams.

John stands at his table and motions for the room to quieten down by moving his arms up and down, hands facing down. When this doesn't work, he shouts, "QUIET!" This has the desired effect; the room goes silent.

"Your leader has an activity on a piece of paper, it is a team activity. I will invite you, in your teams, to go to a separate area in the compound. You can stay in the room if you like but you need to be able to speak to each other and listen to each other. I cannot emphasise enough the need to work as a team, communication is the key to this."

Jason comes over and says, "Where do you want to work?"

"How about in that corner?" Ronan asks, and points to the corner of the room to our right.

"Perfect, come on, everyone." We follow him to the corner and carry a couple of chairs to make the six we need. We sit in a huddle and Jason reads out the instructions on the page.

Metis team – Leader Jason – Tracy, Tina, Ronan, Abbie, Latifa
Skills - *demonstrate communication, turn taking, ability to listen, empathise and support team members.*
Activity – *each member to tell the others three strengths and a weakness that they feel they have.*

"Okay, I'll go first," volunteers Jason. "My strengths?" he pauses. "My weakness is easy; I'll start with that. I am afraid of heights." He smiles at the looks we all gave him. How could he possibly be in a job like this, walking up mountains, abseiling and building bridges, if he couldn't stand heights? "I know, but that leads to one of my strengths, I guess. I try constantly to overcome my fear by putting myself in situations where I am tested. Sometimes it works and sometimes not. It's getting better. The other two strengths are trickier… People say I am kind, I think that is something to be proud of. Oh, and I am good at first aid." He looks at all of us, "Do we have a volunteer to go next?" No one moves. Clearly it is very early in our relationship journey and we don't want to expose ourselves at this stage.

"I'll go," Latifa says. Having watched her in the group, she seems like a quiet girl, unassuming and really intelligent. I heard her say that she goes to a school in Dunstable. I like her. Latifa, pushes her thick black hair off her shoulders, so that it falls against her back, clears her throat subtly and shifts slightly in her chair. "Okay," she says. "My weakness is swimming; I can't do it. Never been for lessons. My parents got me extra maths and physics lessons when I was younger and they were always on the same days as swimming lessons; for my parents, the choice was simple. My dad always said that

I can go into the water or not, but I have to earn enough to survive, to do that, I need qualifications and a good job." She stops, looking guilty. It looks like she feels disloyal to her family, and immediately continues talking, maybe to dilute the negative feelings she is having by talking about her strengths. "I am good at henna tattoos, which might not be so relevant here," she smiles. "I have cooked since being young, helped Mum in the kitchen and she taught me. Although I am not sure I will find the ingredients for pakoras and samosas in the wilderness, I wouldn't mind the cooking detail. My third one is difficult, but I guess I am kind too, if I can replicate that one from you?" She looks at Jason.

"Share with pride!" he says and smiles. "That was great, Latifa. Some great skills there. Loads we can use in the field and don't count any out. Everything is useful. Don't worry about the swimming, I'll be with the group throughout and you won't be in danger. I promise." He smiles at her and she returns his look with a reassured expression. This was clearly on her mind and she had been worrying about it. "Any volunteer to go now, Latifa has made a good start."

"I'll try," I say. Everyone looks at me. I suddenly have no idea what I am going to say, and my mouth is dry. I feel like a performing animal in a circus who has forgotten my routine, the expectant audience wants their money's worth and I have nothing to give.

"Go ahead. Abbie, is it?" Jason says, slowly, as he tries to read my name tag. I realise that a jacket fold is covering it and nod, to negate him searching me to closely to confirm his recollection of my name.

"My weakness... I am lonely. I have friends, really good friends but I miss my brother, so I feel weak. He died you see, and I miss him." Where the hell has that come from? Why did I expose myself to Tracy, to all of them? I hadn't been able to talk about Jamie to Mum, she couldn't handle it and I hadn't wanted to speak too openly to Sky, I never wanted our friendship to change and I think if I banged on about feelings and emotions, it would change things. Maybe I really needed to say it and this is my first opportunity? "I haven't said that before, I am not sure why I just did, but it is true. If it's okay, we will leave that one there. I don't want to discuss it."

Latifa puts her hand on my wrist and squeezed. "Oh bless you, Abbie. I am so sorry. It must be so hard."

I look at her. I know that I am crying as the tears are stinging my eyes and my chin is tickling with the drips of water falling from it. Latifa is crying too.

"It has taken enormous strength to say that, Abbie. We won't pry but if you would like to talk to someone whilst you are here, confidentially, that can be arranged." Jason looks concerned.

"Seriously, I am fine, but thanks." Weirdly, as vulnerable to Tracy's ridicule as I probably am now, showing my true emotions, I feel lighter, like a weight has been lifted. I have said it out loud, that Jamie had died, to strangers no less.

"Abbie, I don't want to pressure you, and it is fine if you don't want to carry on but if you have two other strengths…" Jason asks.

I look at him, I had forgotten that I still had more to say. "Of course, I am fit, I guess that's a strength. I used to play netball and hockey for school." I look at Tracy and surprisingly, the look I get back is not one of contempt, as I was expecting. "But…" I continue, "my foot and ankle were crushed in an accident. I have worked hard on physio and it's nearly as strong as the other one now, although my competitive days are over, apparently." I look at the ground. My fingers tangled in knots on my lap, like tagliatelle in an Italian carbonara.

"I know that your fitness will come in very handy, and a third?" Jason prompted.

"I am loyal, to my friends and family and stuff, I know I need them, and I look after them. It sounds selfish but I would do more for them than I would do for myself." I have finished. God that was hard, much harder than I thought it was going to be. As I was talking about being loyal, the faces of Amber and Paula flashed in my memory. The way that they were talking about Tracy behind her back, how they really felt about her. Did she know? Would she care?

"I think we have time for only one more, today, although the last two will be able to pick this up in the morning, before the first activity," Jason instructs, he then invites either Tina, Ronan or Tracy to speak. To my surprise, Tracy nods and noisily moves her chair, centre stage, I think.

"Well, I have been thinking about my strengths and I think that I would start with my knowledge about fashion. I guess it's not very relevant here, although Stella McCartney has released her new season and there is a conservation theme with leaves and forest motifs on the fabric, so I guess it is relevant." She looks pleased with herself to find the link. I have never really listened to her talk before, but it amazes me how superficial she sounds.

"That's really interesting, maybe if the fashion industry can pay more attention to the need for conservation and become more sustainable, their consumers would take note and the message can get out that we need to take care of the planet?" Jason says, attempting to build on the shallow reference provided by Tracy. When I look at her, she had clearly not thought beyond the look and probable purchase of a jacket. What it is made of, where it comes from, who makes it, under what conditions, are not details that she finds relevant or interesting and her expression makes this obvious.

"Yes well, I guess my next strength would be my number of followers on Instagram and Facebook." She looks pleased and is obviously anticipating the enquiry regarding how many she has. Disappointingly for her, this question doesn't come.

"And your third?" Jason asks, not impressed so far, although, to his credit, he is masking it quite well.

"Oh, ok then," Tracy didn't think that the full explanation for the last strength had been given but she soldiered on. "My third, would be my empathy." I stare at her, what the hell. Empathy? She obviously doesn't know what that means. My face is my downfall and everyone I know says that I don't have to say anything at all, my face can hold a conversation on my behalf as my expressions are transparent and often betray me when I am upset or annoyed. This must have been one of those occasions and I see Jason looking at me, concerned. To avoid any unnecessary interruption from me, he steps in.

"What does empathy mean to you?" he looks at Tracy.

"Well its being nice, understanding, respecting them, if they deserve it," she says. I don't really know what to do with that last statement. She shows me no empathy, is that because she doesn't really know what it means, she doesn't know how to express it or that she doesn't think I deserve any empathy?

Thankfully, John stands up and apologises but says that the activity has run out of time and that it will continue in the morning, so anyone who has not had a chance to contribute can do so.

We are then taken to our cabins by Olivia. She makes sure that we have collected all our equipment from the sides of the canteen building and the girls line up behind her, army style. The boys line up behind Jason. The sleeping areas are segregated, male and female, with no connecting doors. Olivia tells us that there had been connecting accesses in the past but after a couple of incidents of inappropriate behaviour amongst clients, these had to be closed off. I found it a little funny to be called a client: it seems like such a grown-up phrase. As we enter the large open dormitory a few of the girls who obviously know each other, walk up to beds together, hoping to claim adjacent bunks. The beds are small, just about the size of a single bed with a sheet and a duvet. There is a small two-draw cabinet at the right side of each bed, with a small moveable light on the top. There is a large box under each of the beds where our luggage, dirty boots and coats can be stored. The floor is tiled and cold, I wish I had the foresight to have brought my slippers with me.

"You will sleep here tonight and for any other nights that you are not on the night trails, you will be sleeping in here," Olivia explains. "Your bunks will be inspected, and we will expect the whole area around each bed and the bed itself to be kept neat and tidy. Any mess will need to be cleaned up. There will be no boys allowed in this dormitory under ANY circumstances. There is a WI-FI code, which I am happy to give to you as I know that some of your parents may be a little concerned about you being away. Contact them but bear in mind, this is supposed to be about your opportunity to be independent and grow, so the less time you spend on the internet, the better. I don't know if any of you smoke – filthy habit, I hope not – but if you do, you do not do it in here. It is against the law anyway so I would suggest that if you do, stop for a week, it will do you good." She looks disgusted all the way through this. I'm with her, I hate the smell of cigarettes and I know that I will never smoke. I look around for any guilty faces but don't see any. Practiced smokers are probably so good at hiding their habit that it wouldn't be easy to tell; there may be some amongst us.

"It will be lights out at nine o'clock," She continues. There are notes of disdain to this announcement. "Every day will be a busy day, you have heard the schedule, you will need your sleep and by the end of the week, you will be glad when nine o'clock comes around." She pauses and lets this sink in. "Right, get your stuff under your beds and get washed for dinner." Just before she leaves the cabin, she turns and says, "The leaders and teachers will be in the large building, next to the mess hall, in case you have a problem, day or night. Okay?"

Latifa comes up to me at this point. "Can I have the bed next to you? I am on my own and was wondering if you would mind?" she asks.

"No worries. I'm going over there," I point to a bunk as far away from Tracy as I can be. "Are you okay in that one, next to mine?" I ask, pointing at the bed to the left of the one I have chosen.

"That's great, thanks," she says.

We put our stuff away and try to make sure our beds are tidy before we leave. Then we go to the mess hall for dinner.

When I return to the cabin, I get changed and get into bed. It is surprisingly comfortable. I pick up my phone and make sure that the Wi-Fi is switched on and text Mum.

'Hi Mum, got here safely. Journey was okay. Met some nice people, especially a girl called Latifa, she goes to a school in Dunstable but is part of our group. There are other kids from other schools too. My bed is nice, food is good. Are you ok? Text me back if you can. Abbie xx'

I wait for a while for a reply, but one doesn't come so I pick up my journal.

Date: 3rd May

First day of the outward-bound course. BH is here and is in my group! We had to describe ourselves to the group we are in – I'm in METIS. I talked about Jamie and feeling lonely. FFS I don't even know these people and the one person I don't want to hear all that was here. WTF am I doing. Suicide! BH said that she likes fashion – she called that a strength! Shallow bitch. She also said she has empathy. Whatever, I'll be surprised if she can spell it, she def doesn't know what it means. And she said that she only gives empathy to those people who deserve it and she looked at me, like she hated me. I don't remember what I have done. I don't think I did anything but if I did, it must have been awful. Why can't I remember? There's a girl here called Latifa, in my group. She's nice. Tent building tomorrow. Never done that. Remembering what my counsellor had drummed into me about positive mindset, I conclude my journal with, *Challenge, not a chore.*

I check my phone again to see if I have a message from mum, but I haven't, so I lay down feeling more tired than I expected. There are no curtains against the windows and the dark, clear sky is clearly visible through the pane. As I watch the tree branches moving rhythmically across the glass like a moving picture in a frame, the sparkly dots in the sheet of blackness beyond the forest seem to fade and disappear. My eyes close and I drift to sleep.

CHAPTER 14

People Have to Want to Change

The next morning, Olivia wakes us early, about six-thirty. "Come on, get dressed and in the mess hall, for breakfast." It is a rude awakening. Even though I had managed to get to sleep, it was disturbed during the night: I guess it is the different bed, and I am so used to being on my own that a room full of people bothers me much more than I thought it would. It never used to. Jamie was in my dreams again. I see him most nights now, always something similar. He is in a wood and I have to find him. When we played, before the accident, his favourite game was hide and seek and it was funny because his giggling would give him away and most of my time was spent, pretending that I couldn't find him, although his hiding places were always obvious. Recently, his games have been less fun. I feel like I MUST find him, like something depends on it. Really weird, it doesn't make sense. I feel sluggish but get my teeth brushed and dressed in the bathroom, quickly before anyone else goes in there. The need to be able to uncover myself in a room where I am on my own seems more important to me than how tired I am, and I manage to override the desperate fatigue I feel.

Once ready, I see Latifa coming from the sparse and very basic bathroom, dressed and seemingly ready for breakfast. "Shall we go?" I ask her.

"Let's. I wonder what it will be? The dinner was nice last night. Vegetarian sausages, mash and beans," she says. I nod. I had the normal pork sausages, but it was good that other diets were catered for. I remember then that I had to specify on the application form if I had any dietary requirements; I guess not eating pork would be one of those. "Do you know what I just saw, in the bathroom?" she asks, giggling.

"No" I reply. "I dread to think." I giggle too.

"You know that girl in our group, Tracy?"

"Yes, she's in my year at school," I explain.

"Is she a friend of yours?" she asks. I can understand why. I could feel that she wanted to tell me something that would be funny about Tracy and doesn't want to insult her in front of someone who might be upset or worse, tell her what she had said.

"No, she's not a friend. We don't get on. I don't know why exactly, just never have. I don't think I ever spoke to her before she started being nasty to me, but don't worry whatever you say will stay between us, promise. What did you see?" I try to reassure her, and it must have worked as after looking around furtively she continues.

"I was at the sink, brushing my teeth and she was stood next to me. She has literally put a full face of make up on. Foundation, blusher, mascara and lipstick. I don't know where she thinks she is or who she is trying to impress, but why would you?" We both laugh as we remember that today we would be preparing for sleeping in tents, so that we are able to survive on our own on Wednesday night. I know that it will be a testing day and am keen to see how Tracy is going to be able to deal with being dirty and having her expensive, branded clothes covered in mud and brambles.

We have a heavy breakfast – they have truly catered for all tastes, breads, jams, cereals and cooked breakfast. As little or as much as you wanted. Once finished, we are instructed to go back to the cabins and gather the tents, cooking equipment, sleeping bags and groundsheets so that we can all practice the noble art of putting up a tent and making our makeshift bedstead comfortable.

Jason, our leader, stands at the centre of the coach park, along with the other leaders. Instinctively, all the Metis team gather around him. I stand with Latifa. After confirming all of us have our equipment for the day, he instructs us to stay with him and he starts to walk through the trees adjacent to the compound and into the connecting forest. As it is June, there has been little rain and the ground is quite hard and a little dusty in places. The constant cracking and splitting of fallen branches as we tread on them is a continual background accompaniment to the birdsong from high in the forest canopy. It is difficult to see through the trees as they are so dense, but I am sure there is a world beyond these endless bark and brambles.

I talk to Latifa throughout this hike in the forest. We talk about our families. She tells me that she is the only girl in a family consisting of mum, dad and three boys. She is the second eldest and when she is at home, she is expected to do all the household chores and look after her two smaller brothers. Her eldest brother, Ravi, is seventeen and is in college, hoping to become an accountant or businessman. Latifa has said that she wants to do well at school so that she can go to college. Her parents want her to become a doctor, but she is keen to study and learn to be a teacher. It is clear from her expression that she is concerned about letting her family down and disappointing them, and I am somehow grateful that my mum seems uninterested in my studies or ambitions because at least I can't let her down if she has no aspirations for me at all. I tell Latifa about the accident. She looks horrified and I immediately feel guilty. It has become a little too matter of fact for me now, as it happened and I can't change it and I must have said it a million times by now, but I forget that for those not knowing or expecting it, news like that can be shocking. I change the subject and tell her about Sky, explaining that we have known each other since we were small and we seem to have a sixth sense about each other, how we are feeling. Not like me and Jamie, but close friends. She tells me about her best friend, who is called Liz. They haven't known each other for as long as me and Sky have, but seem to have a similar relationship.

After about an hour of walking, where Jason frequently interrupts our conversation by picking up the odd plant, insect and flower and gathering the group together to tell us about their origin, how they germinate and whether they are poisonous, we come to a clearing at the edge of the wood. It seems to spring from nowhere and suddenly the trees stop, and grass takes over. The grass looks untouched, with wild daisies and dandelions covering the wide expanse. It is about the size of a netball pitch, and although there is a slight incline, it is mainly flat. Perfect for tent making, I guess.

Jason demonstrates how to erect a tent by putting his own up in the centre of the clearing. Bending down and examining the ground he begins by explaining the importance of finding an area that is free of large rocks and branches, so that the ground is smooth. I look at the ground around me and it looks grassy and, thankfully, stone free. Jason reminds us that it is summer and if we don't want to roast in the morning, it might be better to find a sheltered spot to allow the tents to warm up gradually. I do think of reminding him that we were in

Wales and the chances of us getting sunstroke or overheating in the morning is close to nil, but I decide just to nod at Latifa and point to a good position under an oak tree at the edge of the forest.

He raises a sheet of tarpaulin and puts it on the area of ground to the left of where he stood, clearly he considers this to be a good area for his tent. Jason then pulls out a black nylon tent bag from his rucksack and opens the tent so that the corners are in similar places on the ground. He returns to the bag and recovers various poles and stakes, placing them next to the tent. Picking up the poles in turn, he shows us the different types of poles that we have. Some are straight pieces of metal, but others have string attaching two poles together. It is a minefield. He demonstrates the art of getting the various shapes of nylon and canvas, gracing the clearing floor to look and act like a tent, by pushing and pulling the different shaped poles through the thin hems of the fabric, attaching the grommets to the stakes to enable the tent to maintain its shape and stability. He tells us that this part is easier with two people, although he manages it in minutes on his own. Practice, I guess. I was hoping that all of us would be asked to work together in our group of five and put up each tent, but it is not meant to be. There is one last piece, a rain fly, which apparently when the paracord is pulled tight, the tent is protected from the rain. Personally, I think that this piece of equipment is much more relevant than the instruction regarding sun protection.

We are let loose on the tents in twos. Me and Latifa work well together, and it seems to be easy. We work on Latifa's tent first. Tracy is with Tina. I didn't know Tina before this trip, she's probably from a different school, but she and Tracy look like they are struggling. Tracy refuses to kneel-down and prefers to give instructions to Tina, who looks stressed and is clearly finding it difficult. Their first tent is only half done when Latifa's is finished. We go on to put up mine.

When all the other tents are put up, the small clearing resembles a camping site. Jason needed to finish Tina's tent as Tracy had refused to help her, as the poles were dirty and she didn't want to run the risk of ruining her new clothes. Exasperated, he knelt-down and fed the poles through Tina's tent fabric and the tent came into being.

Jason invites us all to sit around his tent and have the water and snacks we had brought with us. Once we sit and begin opening the various packets of crisps and chocolate bars he says, "Right, yesterday only four of us managed to give our three strengths and one weakness. As all our strengths have to be pulled together, I think we should give Tina and Ronan an opportunity to tell us what they are good at. Is that okay?" he looks over to both of them, who happen to be sitting next to each other near the door of Jason's tent.

"I'll go first if you like," Tina looks at Ronan and he nods and waved his arm, inviting her to continue. "Okay, my strengths…mmm…I guess my years in Guides and now Rangers might help. We have done some rope knots and fire making although my tent making has always been woeful."

Jason laughs. "Maybe your tent-making does need work, but the other skills will definitely come in useful. Your other strengths?"

"The others, I can sing, not brilliantly but I can. Not that you will see me on the voice or X Factor any time soon, but my cousins all like my singing. My third, I am fit, I can run, I've done lots of half marathons, I take part in the Luton Park Run on a Saturday in Wardown Park. I guess that's my three. My weakness is easy, I can't stand close spaces, we went to Dell Farm near Dunstable with Guides and had to go in caving exercise, I lost it, went bat-shit crazy. The rest of the trip was excellent and everyone else loved the caving, but I was hyperventilating and needed to be taken home."

Jason looks a little concerned but is reassuring in his response to Tina. "Don't worry, if there is a caving type exercise, I will ensure that someone else in the team takes the lead in those, if they don't volunteer."

"I'll do it, I don't mind small spaces and stuff like that," I say.

"Thanks, Abbie," Tina says with an embarrassed smile. She looks relieved.

"Great, well only one more to go, so last but not least, Ronan, are you ready?" Jason asks, grinning at Ronan.

"Okay, I don't have any really useful strengths, I am a gamer. I spend hours on my PlayStation trying to perfect what I do. It's a skill, but I'm not sure it's a strength…"

"Skill?" Tracy said with disdain.

"Moving on. Your other skills, Ronan?" he says, inviting him to carry on and paying no mind to Tracy's opinion.

"Okay," Ronan says, it is clear that Tracy's comment has hit home and bothered him. He tries to regain his composure. "I am an army cadet, although I have only been doing it for about a year, we have been taught a little bit about map reading and using radios. I guess that they might be skills that might be relevant here, but I am not that good at them as we have only practiced once, on camp."

"Really good skills, Ronan, all three of them," he looks at all of us, although his gaze lingers on Tracy. "The map reading, and radio work may come in useful. Don't worry about how little experience you have, you have more than any of your team members probably. To be honest, the PlayStation hobby will provide you with tactics and team play, so there is nothing wasted." He nods at Ronan and he takes this as an indication to continue with his weakness.

"Okay, my weakness, I am asthmatic, so I find a lot of running around and walking up hills really hard, but if I have my puffers, I am fine. Don't worry, I won't die on you and I will still pull my weight." He looks around the group for support.

I look at him, "My best friend, Sky, has slight asthma. I've never seen her having an attack, but she has spoken about them. You can stay with me and Latifa if you like, we'll look after you." I look at Latifa, she nods.

"Cheers," Ronan smiles.

"Great, fab teamwork guys," Jason beams around the team. "Let's check out what you have learned about the forest and tents, part of this course is about you learning to rely on yourselves, both in your teams but also as individuals." We look at each other, a test? I never saw that coming.

Jason then asks us questions about the various plants and insects we saw as we walked through the wood to get to the clearing. When we have provided enough information to demonstrate that we had actually been listening to him and his explanation of what was safe to touch and even eat, he moves on to his questions designed to test our knowledge regarding the best way to put up a reliable tent. Having answered them sufficiently, more as a team than individuals, as I am not sure that any one of us was listening intently enough to be able to recall all the technical terms and what they do, we have lunch.

As the rest of the day is supposed to be preparing us for a night in our tents and being self-sufficient, we have a conversation about the benefit and risk of making fires. How they can be made safely and how they can be used to both keep warm and cook.

We have a few attempts each of setting fires and find that the most proficient, apart from Jason, was Ronan; must be his army training. I make a mental note that I would try and make sure that my tent is near to Ronan's, so that I can get some of the heat from his fire, as mine was pitiful.

After putting our tents down, we have the nightmare chore of getting the tent fabric and poles back in the nylon bag. Tracy ends up throwing hers on the floor and refuses to continue trying to put it in the bag. I've finished mine and am on my way to help her, reluctantly, but catch the look that Jason is giving me. I stop in my tracks and wait to see what he is going to do.

"Tracy, I think that you can do it, I will help you by telling you what to do but it will be much better if you could try and do it on your own." He is patient and quiet in the way he speaks to her. A complete contrast to her reaction.

"I can't do it, I'm telling you, I can't." She doesn't look upset or embarrassed. She just looks annoyed and probably can't believe that someone isn't doing it for her as she has thrown a tantrum. Maybe that's what happens at home?

"We cannot go back until they are all done, you need to do it or ask someone in your team to help you. If you are going to ask them to help, it is to help, not to do it for you, and ask nicely. This is your tent and your responsibility." She looks murderous, her outburst has not had the effect she was expecting, and she is not used to having to ask for anything, it clearly 'just happens.'

I sit with the others on the edge of the clearing. We have positioned our tent bags in a circle and are using them as back rests as we watch the drama unfold around the remaining tent, still erect at the side of the clearing. I'm not expecting Tracy to back down but after about ten minutes, she reluctantly comes over.

"Anyone want to help?" she asks. The closest thing to a polite request that she is capable of, I guess.

"I will," I say, standing up. Tracy looks surprised, as does Jason.

"Me too," Latifa joins us. As she stands up, Tina and Ronan stands up with her and we walk together across the clearing to the tent. As we reach the tent, Tracy seems to step back, allowing us unhindered access.

"I am sure that Tracy meant for you to all work on this as a team, Tracy what bit do you need help with?" Jason recognised the signs of Tracy withdrawing and called her on it. Good on him!

"This," Tracy hands me the nylon bag and seems to be asking me to put the tent and poles away for her.

"If you get the tent folded, I'll hold the bag so you can put the tent in." I open the bag and point the open end towards her.

"It's too hard… God, why do I have to do that?" Tracy says as she bends down. Her tantrum has peaked and is now waning. It looks like she has burned herself out and reluctantly has chosen to comply, not to be part of the team, but because there is no choice.

As a team, it takes minutes to put her tent away and it shows that we can work together. There are no thanks from Tracy, although there had been no expectation of one.

We make our way back to the main compound to have some downtime, get showered and ready for dinner.

CHAPTER 15

Trust Creates a Bond

Olivia's wake-up call is a little unnecessary for me today. I hardly slept although when I went to bed last night I had felt exhausted. The fresh air, I guess. I watched the girls around me fall asleep, one by one but just couldn't switch off. I have no idea why. I don't remember dreaming, for the first time in ages, and I hadn't done my journal, maybe that was it.

I get quickly to my feet, gather the clothes I will be wearing today and my toiletries and run to the communal bathroom and changing room, determined to have the opportunity to change in peace.

Once dressed, I prepare my rucksack for today and tomorrow, knowing that we will be hiking and sleeping out tonight in our tents. I don't know how far we will be walking on our hike, but I make a mental note to ensure that Ronan isn't alone just in case his asthma flares up.

Latifa emerges from the bathroom, excited about the day. I remember that on the itinerary, there was no mention of water-related sports, and being a non-swimmer, she has nothing to worry about. "Where do you think we will be hiking? There are lots of hills and mountains around here, do you think we will be walking up some of those?" She sounds keen to get started. It was great to see her so animated, yesterday she had faded into the background a little with Tracy making such a scene about the tents.

"Probably," I answer. "It would make sense. We wouldn't have to bus there, and we could walk to a hill and up it."

John stands at the front of the canteen. He is trying to get everyone's attention by saying, "Quiet everyone, can everyone hear me?" This, having no effect whatsoever, is abandoned as an option. Having had a rethink, he then favours a loud whistle for which he put two fingers of each hand into his mouth and blows. Success! With a start, everyone turns around. Objective achieved.

"You all need to listen to this; it is vitally important." Once it looks like he has everyone's attention, he continues, smiling. "Should you go into a field where there are sheep or cows during your hike, you must always treat the animals with respect. They were here long before we were, and the farmers have a great relationship with our company. We do not want to put that relationship and all our hard work to get it at any risk. Should I hear that anyone has been rude to any of the farmer's representatives or their family or that anyone has mistreated any of the animals or damaged any property, I will treat the situation with utmost severity." He looks serious, there isn't a sound in the room. As kids from school we know the difference between stuff we think we can get away with and things we really can't. Boundaries are there to be pushed but none of us need to make stupid decisions, we have paid to be here and the majority of us want to get the most out of it. For me, it's an opportunity I never thought I would have, I am not going to mess it up.

Once John has finished his message, he invites us all to gather our rucksacks and equipment. Having retrieved our stuff from the side of the canteen, Team Metis makes our way to the centre of the coach park where we have arranged to meet Jason. Whilst standing there, we begin to discuss tactics, reminding each other of our strengths and weaknesses from the previous couple of days' conversations. I'm pleased to see that although it doesn't appear to be what she wants to do today, Tracy is listening to our conversation, and to some very small effect is joining in the conversation. I wonder if she has turned a corner, if the debacle about the tent building and her prissiness regarding her reluctance to contribute and everyone's reaction to it has resonated with her? Maybe? I'm yet to be convinced that one afternoon can change a person's character to that degree.

Jason arrives with his rucksack and equipment. I notice he has a hefty first aid kit attached by a clasp to his belt.

"Right, shall we go?" says Jason. "Is everyone ready? Ronan, do you have your inhaler?"

"Of course, never go anywhere without it," Ronan says smiling.

Jason is keen to put some footsteps between the compound and our destination. It is clear from the speed in which he start to walk. At some point he seems to check himself, probably reminding himself that he is with a group of teenagers for whom exercise on this scale is not a normal part of our routine. He then starts to slow down. I'm pleased, on Ronan's behalf, as keeping the same pace would be difficult for him to maintain, considering his asthma issues.

We reach the trees of the surrounding wood in less than a few minutes, and then traverse around the tree line which skirts the base of the mountains that we can see from the east side of the compound.

Looking up the side of the mountain that we are just about to walk up, Jason starts to describe what it means to the locals. I can't believe how well he can speak. He sounds like he is out for a daily stroll, not that he is working hard. That could not be said for the rest of us, all of us are breathing hard and stop occasionally to get our breath back. I know that Jason knows this, although he carries on, unperturbed, not stopping to cajole anyone apart from Ronan, who he takes care of.

"This mountain it is," according to Jason, "stuff of local legend." Jason tells us that "Many of the hikers who venture onto this mountain have been lost. Some have never been found and no communication has been received from them since they left their homes the morning of the hike." He doesn't seem to be saying this to scare us, his description is far too matter of fact. He uses this information to explain that it is for this reason that we will do everything in pairs today.

Latifa and I quickly stand next to each other, assuming that we can be the first pair to be drawn, as we seem to have made a natural link since meeting each other. It makes sense to us. We had done so well the day before and even been first in completing the tent-building exercise.

"I have arranged three pairs and they are as follows," Jason tells us. "Abbie will be with Tracy today; Tina will be with Ronan and Latifa will come with me." He carries on, "The pairs are only relevant when there is a situation which requires a pair to take part. This will be rare, and I can't envisage a reason for this, but should it be necessary for our group to be split into smaller groups, that's the pair you will be with, is everyone clear? Does anyone have any issue with the pair they are with?" He looks around the group smiling. I can see that he knows how uncomfortable this is for some of us, especially anyone who is put with Tracy. So why did he choose me? Yesterday, he seemed to know that there was a history between us. If he was aware of this, why the hell would he put me in this position? Doesn't he like me? What have I done to upset him? I rack my brains, but I can't think of anything…

I struggle to lift my head and look at Tracy, I can imagine the look on her face is probably one of absolute disdain and disappointment. However, I don't know who else she would prefer to be with from our group, I definitely can't think of anyone who would volunteer to take my place.

I look at Latifa and can see that she is a little disappointed that she isn't with me, but instead of saying that, she grabs my arm, squeezes it and says to me, "I am so sorry that you got Tracy."

"I know," I reply. "I'm glad you didn't." We both smile at each other, a knowing, shared expression.

During the hike, me and Latifa walk together. We spend the whole time talking about the spectacular views as we walk up the hill. The endless fields of different colours, the yellow of the rape seed bright in large expanses of farmland. In the distance there are countless squares of farmland with green grass dotted with sheep and cows close by and as far as the eye can see. It is amazing, so beautiful.

In Luton, there are the various hills and surrounding fields. In fact, just behind my own house, in Bushmead, there are the Warden Hills which stretch all the way to Lilley and in the other direction, to Barton. Only ten minutes' walk into those hills it is easy to forget that I live in an urban area such as Luton. The views from Warden Hills, although beautiful, pale into insignificance when I look at the incredible scene in front of me.

As the hike continues, both me and Latifa keep an eye on Ronan. His breathing seems a little laboured but okay and we both make a pact to look after him throughout this walk.

"In that direction, is Anglesey," says Jason. He points to his left. We all look round and try and see in the distance an island which is unfortunately just out of view and lost in the mist which covers the view around the horizon. Jason continues to tell us who the farmer is who owns the field that we are walking in. He explains that it's a man that they know as farmer Evans.

Jason points in the direction of a small structure in the distance. "He lives in a grey stone building, over there" I look in the direction that he is pointing and see the building, just about visible. It is a single-storey building at the centre of an expanse of separate fields surrounding it. There is a main road which links this farmhouse to the outside world. An essential part of any commercial business in this rural area of North Wales. Apparently, the outward-bound compound has a great relationship with Mr Evans, and he and his wife supply all of the meat for the various groups who attend. So, the bacon and eggs that were served in the morning for breakfast came from the animals on their farm.

The air is warm, and I need to take my jacket off, partly due to the changing and warming weather we are lucky to have, but also because of the energy we are using to walk. I take off my jacket, newly bought from Primark, at the mall when I went shopping with mum prior to the trip. Using the sleeves, I tie it tight around my waist so that my rucksack is not hindered by the additional clothing on my bottom half.

It's about an hour later when Jason finally allows us to stop for lunch. We have been given packed lunches to carry by all the leaders at the beginning of the hike, and now it appears to be the time that we can finally open them and eat the contents.

Latifa has a special pack with a V written on the paper bag. indicating a vegetarian meal. As we sit on the side of the hill looking at the scenery, it is amazing how small the compound looks from where we were. It looks like we've walked tens of miles when in truth it's probably only about a mile and a half, although the compound looks so small in the distance.

The sandwiches are okay and the ham I had was probably from the farm, along with the eggs from the egg mayonnaise Latifa had. The sandwiches are accompanied by crisps and a chocolate bar. Mine is a Twirl, Latifa has a Mars Bar and we all have been given a plastic bottle of water. Hard to be sustainable under these circumstances.

Unfortunately, having eaten our food, we have to carry packaging around with us until we can find a bin which I guess won't come until the end of our journey. That is, unless there is a bin at the top of the mountain that we are walking up. Sometimes there is a café at the top of tourist attractions, although I don't know how well-known this mountain is and whether it qualifies as a tourist attraction. I know that when I climbed Snowdon, with my dad, there was a café at the top where we could get rid of the wrappers from the chocolate bars that we had eaten on our way up. In truth, this mountain really doesn't compare to Snowdon, so I am not hopeful. It would be good to get rid of any excess baggage, as I think that this hike may feel like a long way by the end of the day.

"Tina and Ronan, could you move forward and check out the stile at the top of this part of the hill, please," Jason asks.

"Course. You ready?" Tina asks Ronan.

"Yeah, let's do it," Ronan says. They then move forward to the top of the view we have. The mountain seems to have a ledge, that we, below it, cannot see beyond. Tina and Ronan walk just a little faster than the rest of us and disappear after a few minutes, on to the ridge and out of our view.

"The stile is here, and it is fine," Tina shouts back from beyond our view.

"Great, thanks." Jason says. "Come on, the view from just past the stile is incredible."

We make our way, following the path already trod by Tina and Ronan. As we reach the stile we find both sitting on a mound of grass adjacent to it. Their expressions are curious. They are pointing behind us and it isn't until we get all the way to the stile before we can see what is capturing their attention. As I turn around, I draw in my breath. The range of colours are amazing, stretching for miles and miles in all directions.

"Oh My God, would you look at this?" I say, to no one in particular.

"I know," says Jason. "I have worked at the compound for years, but I never get used to this view. It's gorgeous isn't it."

Looking in the direction of the remainder of the mountain, I can see that we are more than halfway up the hill now, a relief for everyone, I think.

"This is a great place to look around. There are lots of holes and crevices around the middle part of this mountain. Feel free to look around, but we are only going to be here for an hour and then we must get to the top and over the other side so that we can get the tents up before nightfall. You all struggled to build your tents in the daylight, I dread to think what a mess you'll make in the dark. We want them livable, don't we?" Jason is laughing.

I giggle and look at Latifa. She is laughing too. We are both dreading the tent-making. We had done okay, but it was not our favourite part of the course.

I start walking to the left of the mountain with Latifa, as the view looked fab. To my surprise, Tracy walks up to me.

"I want to walk this way too and as we are partners you have to come with me," she tells me.

I look at her and then back at Latifa, "I'm sorry, mate." I am disappointed, I would much rather spend this time with Latifa. What a nightmare.

"That's okay, Abbie, look after yourself and don't let her push you around," she says.

"Don't think I've got much choice, she doesn't know any other way, unfortunately," I say, eyes pointed at Tracy. "See you in a little while, you will tell Jason?"

"I guess so, laters." Latifa waves half-heartedly.

"Are you coming?" Tracy asks, although I know in truth it's a rhetorical question.

"Alright..." I say and follow her into what looks like a shallow cave in the side of the mountain. As I walk into the cave, it obviously goes into the mountain a lot further than it looks at first glance. As we walk in, beyond the area that the sun reaches, it is noticeably colder and there seems to be a draft from further in the cave. As the opening is quite tall, we are both able to stand up, however, as we walk into the darkness, the height is as absent as the light. From in front of me, I hear Tracy shout out as she obviously hit her head on the descending ceiling of hard mud and rock.

"You okay?" I ask. "What's happening up there?"

"The ceiling's low, so I banged my freaking head." She takes a deep intake of breath. "There is a fork in the tunnel, left, or right?"

"I can't believe you're asking me that; we have gone too far already. We need to go back; they'll all be looking for us." I say. "Come on, that's enough. We're not going to see any more if we go any further." I say. It is clear from my tone that I have had enough, and we need to return to the others, but I know that this is not even going to register on Tracy's interest scale.

"Come on, scaredy-cat, or do you need a saucer of milk?" she said with the utmost nastiness.

"I was surprised that you would have wanted to come down here at all, with your hate of dirt and mud. Why did you want to come down here in the first place?" I ask.

"I just did, and where I go, you have to come!" she says.

"So, its control, that's all it is with people like you… I knew it."

"What does it matter to you? It's not like you have any clothes you can't get damaged, your whole outfit costs as much as one of my shoes," she says with venom. I cannot see her, but I can hear the smile on her face.

I hear some movement up ahead and then a scream, a sound of sliding and then a noise like a huge bag of flour being dropped in a bowl of mud.

"Oh my God, I've broken my leg. I'm going to die down here and it's your fault." She is screaming. I can't understand most of what she was saying.

"Wait here and I will go and get help." I try my phone and can't get a signal. I knew it was difficult in the London Underground, so it's probably impossible here, for a similar reason.

"So, you are going to leave me in a mess, like father, like daughter," she says.

This brings me up short. "What did you mean by that?" I ask, incredulously. What the hell was she talking about? How does she know my dad? What did he do? "Tracy, what did you say?"

"You know exactly what I am talking about. Don't pretend. You play thick really well, but I know you know more than you're saying," she says. There are some groans and she has clearly hurt herself and I should go for help, but I can't let this conversation go.

"I really don't know what you're talking about. What about my dad? Did you know him? What are you talking about?" I ask.

"He didn't mention my name?"

"No, really. Should he have?" I ask. "Is that why I was summoned here?"

"No, I assumed he had and that you knew. I was waiting for you to tell everyone at school," she almost whispers this sentence. This is a mystery now. What could dad know about Tracy that I didn't? Unless it was something about his work, because he couldn't tell us. I assumed that this must be it.

"Even if I knew, whatever it is you think I know, I would never tell anyone." I think about this quickly. "What is it? Do you want to talk about it?" I wonder how many people she has told, and whether, a little like my disclosure on my first day, she needs to clear the air and open-up. Maybe the option to talk about it in the safety of a cave, with someone who promises to keep the secret may be what she needs to help her get over the worry of the secret being exposed. I guess that's what I needed to do when I arrived at the course. If I have the control of how the story is told, it remains my story. I could do the same for her.

"I haven't told anyone before. I think that Amber and Paula would take the piss and tell everyone they know. Why did you tell us all about Jamie and how lonely you feel? Why would you do that in front of me, I wouldn't have done that," she asks.

"I needed to own it. It has been an absolute nightmare losing Jamie, but I have to take control of it, tell who I want to tell, in the way that I want them to hear it. The fact that I have lost Jamie won't change but I have only told those I want to hear it. It's too precious to let everyone know. You can do the same, if you are ready to," I explain, sincerely. To my surprise, she begins to speak about the worst experience of her life.

"It was when I was eleven. Before I came to high school. I was on my computer, speaking to friends on Skype, in my bedroom and there was a pop-up advert, inviting interest in a competition where a year's supply of fashion clothing was the prize. It sounded too good to be true. I clicked on it. I didn't want to lose the opportunity to have the fashionable clothes. So, when I clicked on to the advert, another window opened and there was a young man on the screen, who obviously using my webcam to see me. I had been using it to talk to my friend. During the conversation we had, he convinced me that I should be a fashion model. I was eleven, the bastard," she says.

"What happened then?" I ask, ashamed to say that I am curious.

"Well…" I can hear that she was nervous, this is obviously the difficult part. My assumption had been correct. I knew that it had to be quite serious for my dad to have been involved. She continues, "Well, he said that I should take my top off and that it was important that he could see how I looked from all angles. To make it easier, he took his top off as well and asked me not to laugh at him as he was shy… Absolute bastard. I took off my top. Abbie, I was eleven. I had just started developing and do you know what he was doing?" she asks.

"What?" I already knew, as my dad had been warning me about things like this from the moment that I got a computer, but I thought that Tracy actually needed to say it out loud.

"He was taping me. The bastard was taping me. He then sent me an email and told me that if I didn't send money and more tapes, he would send the video to everyone on my address list and post it to YouTube." She takes a breath; I think that the whole disclosure is in one go. Maybe she needs to say it before she loses courage.

"What did you do?" I asked.

"I had to speak to my mum, she was horrified. When my dad was told, he said that he was disappointed, I wish he had shouted at me. He said we had to get the police involved. I begged him not to as they had said that if we went to the police, they would post the videos. I was petrified." She says, slightly shouting now.

"Did the police get involved?" I can now see where my dad comes into the story.

"Yes, a DC Carter came in to see us. James Carter, is that your dad?" she asks.

"Yes…" I say.

"Well, at first, he was really interested and came to see me. Gave mum and dad loads of chat about working out where the originating computer and user come from, that it was going to be a long process and that the person probably comes from a different country, it was really hard to get a conviction, how much he cares blah, blah, blah…" She was angry almost ranting. "But did he really care? Who knows, he never spoke to us after a while. Didn't once contact us." She sounded exasperated.

"When was this?" I asked, trying to pinpoint the timings, clarifying the sequence of events.

"Three years ago, I was eleven remember…" she says, a little sarcastically.

"I think that my dad cared too much. He left all of us because he couldn't help you. My dad was a police officer on cybercrime and was always telling us how difficult it was to investigate the cases and how few cases actually go to trial. Nothing to do with him, all about the offenders being in different countries and websites being taken down as soon as they had been rumbled. He was never allowed to speak about the cases he was running at home, but I know that they all upset him. He cared so much about the victims, who were nearly always children. I guess it was worse because he had children too," I explain.

"What do you mean, he left all of us? Did he walk out on you?" she asks.

"No, mum got home one day, and he had hung himself in the garage, it was awful. I felt like my life had ended as well." I can feel tears falling down my face and am glad of the dark, for the first time since we walked into the cave.

"Jesus, when was that?" Tracy asks.

"Three years ago, in August."

"Oh my God, my investigation started in June. Do you think I had anything to do with it?" she asks. Her voice is sincere, but how could she think that she was responsible?

"I think that your case was one of many where he felt that he couldn't help the victims. It was too much for him to deal with. It wasn't fair. Our whole family changed. Mum was a different person, Jamie had grief counselling and we lost most of our money as dad had been the biggest earner. Since then, we have struggled to make ends meet." I think I have nothing to lose now. I am not telling her off or being cruel, but a fear of humiliation is not the worst thing in the world that could happen to someone. Only the worst thing that can happen to someone like her.

"Oh my God, I hated you, I thought you knew, and you could destroy me," she says, probably as a justification for being such a bitch for so long.

"But I didn't, and if I did, I wouldn't have said a word. Why would I? One thing you should know is that people are less likely to be cruel to you if you are nicer to them. You really do need to try it," I say.

"Tracy, Abbie, are you down there?" I hear Jason shouting from the mouth of the cave.

"Yes, down here, to the right of the fork. I couldn't leave Tracy, she fell over," I shout back. "Are you okay now? Can you walk, do you think?" I ask her, I know that I am sounding slightly impatient, but I need to get out of the cave and back into the fresh air.

CHAPTER 16

The Missing Boy

Jason is relieved to find both me and Tracy in the cave. With difficulty, we manage to extract Tracy. For all her groaning and moaning, on examination, her ankle is only slightly sprained. She had obviously caught it on a rock as she slid down the muddy bank in the darkness.

As we reach the daylight, the conversation that we shared in the cave creates an uncomfortable knowledge about each other and a definite atmosphere of nervousness.

The saying what happens in the cave stays in the cave, (a slight amendment to the original obviously), is really relevant here. We cannot unhear what we had heard, nor can we take it back. Our shared secrets create a debt of respect and confidentiality, and both of us know that we have to trust each other to keep what was said between us.

For me, things have changed. The conversation has created a context for the animosity, and I can understand the justification that Tracy would have put on her behaviour and attitude towards me. That isn't to say that I agree with her reaction, or the way she has treated me for those three long years, but I can understand why she felt that she could. She had stated that she did not think I deserved any respect or empathy from her, was this still the case?

As I feel the breeze on my face, the outside air smells sweeter than I remember. This feels a little dramatic considering we had only been in the cave for probably half an hour, tops.

Latifa comes running towards me and asks, pointedly, "Are you okay?"

I reply, "Yes, of course, actually I'm fine really." And I am. In fact, I feel a lot more relaxed than I have for some time, to be honest.

Latifa explains that the four remaining Metis team had been searching for us since we went in the cave. She says that although she had a feeling about where she had lost us originally, she could not pinpoint our location, so they were all concerned that we had fallen down the mountainside.

The fresh clear air, although a blessing, has also brought into focus the state of our clothes. We recover ourselves and brush ourselves off. Remarkably, Tracy seems a little less concerned about her filthy Victoria's Secret anorak, which obviously would cost a fortune but is now covered, front and back, in mud and silt from inside the mountain.

As me and Latifa walks back towards the stile, Jason calls me back and asks to speak to me. His expression is serious and concerned and his tone is a similar one to the disappointed tone my mum uses when she is upset with me. "Why didn't you come to the mouth of the cave, and shout for help?" he asks.

I feel like I am on trial, speaking on my own defence, I tell him that I was about to come out and call but as I turned away from Tracy, who was walking in front of me in the cave, I heard her scream. She had slid down the internal cave side and was moaning about her ankle. I knew she might be hurt, and she was definitely scared. When I had told her that I was going to have to leave her to get help, she begged me not to leave her. So, I stayed with her and tried to calm her down. My thought was to try and make her comfortable, so that it would enable me to eventually seek help. I couldn't go and leave her at that time, she was a mess. I had been concerned about her, but I know that I needed to convince Jason, how dire the situation felt and the awful decision I had to make.

He considers this explanation for some time and then smiles. Thankfully he seemed happier with this account. He nods and taps me on the shoulder, with an expression of understanding. "You did a brave thing, Abbie. Real teamwork. Well done."

Following my conversation with Jason, Latifa, who is walking just behind us, re-joins me. We continue our walk to the stile, during which I explain that me and Tracy chatted about ordinary things whilst in the cave. Latifa is clearly concerned about me being alone in her company for that length of time and wants to know that she didn't do anything to me. Although I am not entirely sure what she would think Tracy is capable of, inside a mountain. I have already made the decision that I am not going to divulge the conversation that had really taken place – that would be wrong, and I would not appreciate that either. Latifa asks me to describe the cave in great detail, she has obviously never been in a cave herself. So, I spend a great deal of time narratively walking Latifa through the cave, piece by slimy piece. The slippery floor, the drip sounds from the distance. The absolute darkness, darker than any dark night or unlit bedroom. The fork in the cave, choosing between two impossible tunnels. Never has there been a more ridiculous choice. The sound of Tracy falling and the dread of having to pull her out of that place, knowing that it would be too much for me and we may have to stay in there. Her eyes are wide during this explanation and her appreciation makes my tone even more melodramatic, although the description of events is authentic, I can't help maximising the possible danger and risk for dramatic effect.

We climb the stile and walk a little further up the hill. Time is getting on and I feel that we need to make our way up the mountain. Due to our mishap, Tracy and I have imposed a delay in the proceedings and have made our conquering of the summit difficult in the time remaining at best. Tracy, Tina and Ronan join us as we continued upwards. The conversation remains on the recent exploits in the cold, dark cave and the distance which seems to have grown between us and Jason becomes noticeable. I turn to try and see why he isn't with us and where he is and see him, walking in our direction, although slowly and around ten metres behind us.

Jason's phone rings, as it has never rung before the sound of the ringtone surprises us all. Irrespective of distance, I think that the human psyche is attuned to hearing ringtones. It may be that we have now evolved to listen out for them as part of our human self-survival mechanism, a little like a mother animal can hear and identify the cry of her own offspring and a baby penguin can identify its own parents call in a freezing landscape of hundreds of adult penguins, all calling for their children.

Jason stops to take the call. We move closer to join him, not wanting to continue up the mountain without him and end up in a separate team again. Even though we can only hear one side of the conversation, it is clearly a concerning discussion taking place.

"What do you mean?" Jason asked. "What, around here? How old? Okay, what does he look like? Blonde hair, only what? Eight years old right. What was he wearing? Blue jumper; sky blue jumper, blue jeans yes, with pale turn-ups. Yes. Grey trainers. Okay, any idea what his name is? His name is Thomas? Okay, Thomas. When did he go missing? Four hours ago. Okay, where about? Around here? On the mountain range? Are there any medical issues that we need to be aware of? Okay, no worries we will keep an eye out. Yeah sure. No worries here. How are you and your team? Yes, thanks John, speak later, mate."

"Okay team, did you hear that?" Jason asks.

"Yeah," we all confirm. I wonder if this is going to be a task, a quest that they always do for the kids on these courses. A way of bonding the team with a common goal. Would they do that with something so serious? What if it's not that? What if its real and there is a little boy, only a year younger than Jamie, alone on the mountain? How scared would he be? Oh my God, we have to find him. Where are his parents? How could they have let him out of their sight? It was scary enough for two fourteen-year old's together in the cave, imagine being half our age and on your own. They wouldn't do that, they know my history or at least Jason does, he wouldn't involve us if it wasn't real, would he? How sick would that be?

In answer to my internal queries, a rescue helicopter flies above and appears to be concentrating on the sides of the mountain, disappearing for a while to our right, whilst it scopes the side we have yet to traverse, then reappearing on our left and hovering above and behind us.

It is awful. As a team, we want to help. Jason gives us a long description of Thomas, the eight-year-old boy, it seems everyone in our vicinity is looking for.

The only sound louder than the helicopter blades is the shouts from the people on the mountain, encouraging Thomas to 'come home' telling him that his dog, Frankie, is missing him and needs him to take him for a walk.

"This is heartbreaking," says Tina. "That poor boy, all alone. We have to do something. Jason, what can we do? Can we be part of a search party?"

"Yeah, can we?" Ronan asks.

"We haven't been asked to and John has said that we need to get to our camp site rather than become embroiled in all of this, if we can. We have a responsibility to protect all of you, so I need you to stay with me and make sure I know where you all are. We don't know why he has gone missing or if there is anything more sinister involved, so let's just make sure that all of you stay safe and if we see him on our travels, we will radio it in. There is nothing stopping us from keeping a sharp look out whilst we make our way though." Jason is as concerned as the rest of us, but I can understand his point of view. Like a babysitter needs to watch their charges, he needs to make sure that our safety is paramount, or OUR parents would have something to say. The fact that another child has gone missing wouldn't even register if one of us got hurt in an effort to try and find him.

"I guess so," I say.

We walk up the mountain, looking around with every step to see if there is a flash of blue from a small jumper or jeans, anywhere in our eyeline. Throughout the trek, we check in with each other but no sign of him is seen. Occasionally, one or other of us shouts his name, there is a slight echo developing as we climb as unbeknownst to us, there is a small range of hills behind the one we are climbing and our voices seem to be bouncing off these and rejoining us in quieter repeats.

The journey up the mountain is long but strangely, with our attention taken completely away from the strain and length of the walk, it feels like no effort at all. Before long, we are at the top of the mountain and able to look around at the three-hundred-and-sixty-degree view. Oh my God, it is beautiful. The wind is slightly strong at the top, but it is warm. The fields in the mid and long distance seem almost colourless but the range of colours in those in the foreground provides the palette which I can transpose. To the north, there is mist in the distance and the cloud cover is a little thicker and it appears to be coming towards us.

Looking down the mountain sides in all directions, the elevation looks gradual. It would make a great slope to sledge down in the snow, but I am not sure I would be able to stop before reaching the bottom, but the rush would be incredible. I could feel another crushed ankle coming on, should I try it. Probably won't.

"Does anyone need a rest? We can wait for a while if anyone needs to," Jason asks. I know it was directed to Ronan, but he said it generally, which was nice. I remember the 'special' treatment that my teachers thought they were giving me in providing me specific chairs, more time, increased access and worst of all, a babysitter, when my leg was damaged, and I was on crutches. In an effort to be kind, they did no more than highlight the issue to the other kids and it led to teasing and proper bullying from Tracy and her cronies. Not to mention poor Stacy, who had to miss her own breaks to escort me around to my lessons in the quiet of the uninhabited corridors in between lessons, when she should have been with her own friends. My teachers could learn a lot from Jason.

There is no request from anyone in the group for any extra time to recover at the top of the mountain, so Jason starts the trek down the other side. It is strange but walking up is a lot easier than walking down. The descent seems to put a lot of pressure on my knees and my left leg was burning, so painful. We are walking north and are leaving the brighter sun behind us. The clouds I had seen a little earlier seem to have gathered speed and are now almost directly above us.

"We need to get a wriggle on," Jason tells us. "I don't think anyone wants to have to erect the tents in the rain and it looks like there is some coming. The clearing for the tent building today is in that copse of trees over there." He points to the left, where there was a mini forest, the trees seem to sit on the side of the mountain providing a natural canopy. I'm dubious as to whether we would be able to locate an area flat enough for us to build tents on that piece of land.

We make our way in that direction, as we are walking, we pass several people frantically looking for Thomas, shouting his name and whistling. The mountain rescue team run past in their fluorescent coats and with their tracker dogs, noses intently sniffing the ground, searching desperately for any sign of Thomas. I wonder if his parents had provided the dogs with a piece of clothing with his scent on it as a comparison to the multitude of smells they were going to come across; to help them identify Thomas from the rest.

Tracy gets to the wood before any of us. I wonder if she wants to show willing, after her charade during the tent building on the previous day.

"Come on," she shouts. Beckoning us towards her.

"Well done, Tracy, lead the way" Jason shouts. Jason takes up the rear, probably making sure that we all make it the woods safely. "Just over here," Jason points to the right of the trees and begins taking the lead. "Watch the branches and roots sticking up, make sure you don't trip up. There is less light now and some of them are more difficult to see." As he is saying this, he points to the ground and as if to demonstrate the point, I am watching him and trip on a root emerging from the ground, from a huge tree on my right. I fall to the ground heavily but thankfully, it is only my pride that is bruised, and I get up, probably a little quicker than I should, needing to catch my balance using the offending tree. As I stand supported, I am surprised that the person who is brushing me down is Tracy, I had expected it to be Latifa and say, "Thanks mate," not realising it is not her.

Tracy replies, "No worries, did you hurt yourself?"

"Not really." I readjust my rucksack so that it is comfortable again and say, "Thank you."

I look over to Latifa and see her surprised and flummoxed expression. I shrug my shoulders in a 'dunno' kind of way.

"You okay, Abbie?" Jason asks.

"'Course, lets go," I say, keen to get going and tackle the tents prior to the rain and the dark coming. Remarkably, we all, including Tracy, who appears to have benefitted from a character transplant since our near burial in the side of the mountain, begin working as a team to erect the tents as fast as possible. It is amazing how we self-determine our own roles during the process and then how these roles, become interdependent and cohesive, enabling the tents to be lined up within half an hour. Fully formed and each secure with all the pegs and grommets in place and tethered correctly.

"Fantastic work, Metis." Jason has an expression like, 'my job here is done' and it doesn't escape me that this is the first time that he has used our team name to congratulate our ability to work together on a project and have a successful outcome.

We then take some time to individually place our sleeping bags in our tents, making sure that we have the insides of the mini canvas bedrooms as comfy as we can, bearing in mind how cold and wet it was likely to be during the night.

I look at Latifa, smile and then say, to no one in particular, "We'll go and get some firewood before it all gets too wet to burn." Latifa takes the hint and follows me into the woods adjacent to the clearing where our tents stand. The ground outside the clearing, even where the trees were that overhung it, is a gentle slope. Not so much of an incline that you would be out of breath by walking up the hill but certainly not flat. There are lots of tree roots exposed, probably where the ground had been washed away during the rain or storms hitting the mountain and running down the sides. The roots and branches create hazardous risks to ankles and I am careful to watch every step to ensure that I am going to be able to join in the following days activities, as the wet day is the day I was most looking forward to. I am mindful not to say this out loud though, as I remembered

Latifa's fear of the water, and it wouldn't be fair to harp on about something that she is probably dreading.

"Watch yourself through here, loads of branches and stuff sticking up," I say, pointing at some offending roots to my right.

"Yeah, thanks. Was there a reason why you wanted to come in here and collect firewood? You don't seem like the arse...onist type," Latifa asks. We both laugh. I suppose it is because we are tired, and she had said the word arsonist really slowly, so the first syllable was really pronounced. Either way, it tickled us, and we laugh like little school kids.

"No, not the arse...onist type," I say. "We just haven't had a chance to catch up, what about this little kid going missing on this mountain. Awful isn't it? I bet his parents are frantic." I don't know why but I just can't get poor Thomas out of my head. Here we are, making sure we are warm and comfortable and for all we know, he is hurt somewhere and can't get any help from anyone. Cold, wet and hungry...

"It doesn't bare thinking about," Latifa replies, shivering. She bends down to pick up some wood from the forest floor. "Do you think that this will be dry enough to burn?" she asks.

"Do I look like Bear Grylls?" I ask her, smiling.

"Well, I think you're a bit taller but other than that, you're the spit of him," she says, we both laugh.

Latifa's phone pings, she looks down. "Mum," she says. "Worried about our safety on a mountain where the boy has gone missing." I nod.

"I expect that the news has gone viral and it's probably on the BBC six o'clock broadcast, so all the parents may know by now. I expect we will all get similar texts, what are you going to say?" In truth, I'm not sure that my mum will know, she was never one to watch the news and only used her phone for Candy Crush and texting me to tell me to hurry home when she needed something.

"I don't know, I mean, the boy is eight. If he has been snatched, the people who do that, generally target specific age groups, don't they? And specific genders? The paedo was probably into young boys, not mid-teen girls. I think we're safe. Anyway, if anyone came near me or you, I would kick them in the nuts."

"Thanks, mate," I reply, smiling. "With my ankle how it is right now, especially after the walk down that hill, I don't think I would make an impression, wherever my kick landed and if I kicked with my right leg, leaning on my left, I would most likely fall over." I feign falling over and Latifa catches me.

"Steady there, Bruce Lee!" she said, laughing.

We carry on selecting the driest branches we can find, flicking off insects and pulling away remaining leaves, before stacking them in a small pile near the foot of a large oak in the centre of the forest.

"Latifa, Abbie, where are you?" Jason is calling. He sounds curious rather than concerned. I'm pleased with this distinction as it shows that he trusts us to be alone and not be stupid.

"Just coming," I shout back. I tap Latifa's arm and head back to the wood pile. "We have collected wood for the fires." We both bent down and picked up a few logs each and made our way back to the clearing.

We took the wood back to the campsite.

"Excellent! Well done. It is going to be really cold tonight so we will definitely need these."

Jason greeted us with open arms. But instead of filling them with the wood we had brought we put the wood on the floor near his tent so that we could then use it to create the bonfire that was starting to become desperately needed in there.

The sun has disappeared and the clouds from the north that we had seen gathering as we climbed the mountain have now staked their claim on the area and created the ominous celestial landscape that we look up on. As a team, we work hard to create a large bonfire, being mindful that we have to keep some of the wood back, to replenish the fire as the night draws on.

The rain that had threatened has not yet transpired, so we are determined to make the most of the opportunity of this respite to fix our food and socialise, Thomas, the missing boy being the main subject of conversation.

We establish from Jason that the other teams are doing very similar things to us and there are alternate mountains around the campsite that they all walked up today. We can envisage them sitting around their own bonfires with similar conversations taking place, Thomas can't be far from anyone's thoughts.

Jason disappears into his tent and brings out a mini frying pan, packets of sausages, and three easy-open tins of baked beans. I have no idea where he was storing them during the walk up the mountain. I never saw any sign of a frying pan or food and don't even remember hearing them clink or clatter against any of his other equipment.

After eating our fill of sausages and beans, we manufacture desert by eating the remaining Mars Bars and Twix we had stored in rucksacks like hibernating squirrels. I manage to forage in my bag from home to find my Mars Bar this morning and now we are glad of the sugar that this provides. We talk as a team about our families and how they have been concerned about the boy going missing and the danger that we may be in by continuing our track on the mountainside. A couple, including Ronan's and Tracy's parents, had specifically mentioned the danger of staying in individual tents on the campsite and the possibility of being snatched from our tents as we slept.

I fail to tell them all that I have received no texts. What could it contribute to the conversation? I think, hope, that had my mum contacted me, the conversation we would have had would have probably been similar to the discussions had by the others with their families, so I join in and contribute to the conversation in the affirmative, agreeing with the concerns and sentiments of their parents. There is a minor sense of loss and even abandonment in this desolate place; to have no word from home feels very desperately lonely irrespective of the fact that I am surrounded by people.

"There is no point in trying to alter anything that you cannot change." This is something that my counsellor had emphasised throughout our sessions. Especially, when I had brought up the loss of Jamie, the need to see him, and the wish that I could take his place or at least be with him. My counsellor would say words to that effect in an attempt to empower me to take control of the life I have. My need to develop this sense of control, I guess, is part of the reason that I was determined to come on this trip. For me to explore strengths I may be unaware that I have and to expose and eradicate the demons I am struggling to rid myself of.

Is my mum trying to make me more resilient by failing to contact me, as other parents have? Or is she clueless of the impact that her absence of communication has, in relation to the neglect experienced by her fourteen-year-old daughter, who is sitting in a cold damp campsite in an area where an eight-year-old boy is missing? Whilst all around her, the parents of her teammates are talking about their concern for them. I am not feeling sorry for myself but am now feeling quite angry about the lack of contact from her. I have received nothing. Doesn't she care about me? Is she okay? Oh no, what if she isn't and they haven't told me because they don't want to scare me? They would have told me if anything had happened to her, wouldn't they? She wouldn't leave me all alone, she wouldn't leave me as well, would she?

"What do you think? Abbie, what do you think?" Jason's question brings my attention back to the group. Lost in my thoughts I had faded out of the group and was not aware of the conversation that had been taking place in my absence.

"I'm sorry, what do I think about what? I zoned out for a minute," I say and look at Jason confused.

"I was talking about the camp and how much easier it was for you to build it as a team," Jason explains. He is smiling, his conversation is clearly to re-engage me in the team and it had been obvious to him that I was mentally in another place.

"It's stonking," I say, trying to drum up enough passion to satisfy him that I am engaged and enthusiastic. "Clearly, working together works, I think we all knew that, but it was difficult at first because we were so new to each other. I think it's hard but sometimes you have just got to forget things about yourself, to find where you fit; a bit like a cog in the wheel or a spoke in a wheel." I struggle to recall the proverb, if it is one. "I can't remember the saying, but a bit like that." I use my hands to try and describe the linkage of wheels and cogs inside the makings of a clock and how they fit together enabling each other to turn to try, demonstrating the interdependency of the different spokes.

Jason nods; he is smiling. "I think you're right and now that you have all found your feet, it's time to use them and get into your tents. You can get changed if you wish, whether you change your clothes or not, it is essential that you get warm. Take this time to contact your parents. Unfortunately, you'll have to use 4G as there is no Wi-Fi here, obviously, but it would help them if you were all to contact them, to say that you are safe. I don't know your religious preferences but please pray if you do and have a really good night sleep. I will be waking you at six-thirty, in the morning. I know it's early." He responds immediately to our groans. "It is vital that we have time to put the tents away and have breakfast, so we can set off on our journey back to the compound. Then we can get ready for the 'wet day' tomorrow. Is everyone looking forward to that?" He asks as he looks around the group.

I can see that he is expecting the majority to be excited. I have to say that his memory is impressive, because he looks at Latifa with some concern. "Don't worry, Latifa," he says, "I will keep an eye on you, and nothing will happen that you don't want to happen." As he says this, he smiles at her in a very considerate way. My teachers could definitely learn from him, I must have thought this about 200 times a day since I met him, but he is great with people.

Latifa smiles. "Don't worry," she says. "I'll be fine, they will need someone to carry the life jackets." She smiles and we were all still giggling as we stand up and go to our individual tents.

As I lay in my tent, listening to the creaking and zipping of other tents around me, I decide to keep on my daytime clothes. I had brought my pyjamas with me to change into, but I consider how futile it is to take off warm clothes and put on cold clothes. I decide against it, in favour of maintaining the warmth I have built throughout the day and attempting to create a cosy sleeping bag. Listening to the beating wind surrounding the tents, I envisage a freezing cold night ahead.

I lie and think about the day. I consider the complete U-turn in Tracy's character; how helpful she has been today in setting up the tents in comparison to yesterday and her petulant tantrum when the prospect was that her new clothes would get dirty. The weirdness of her wanting me to go in the cave with her. I know that we were designated as partners, but it still felt very contrived for her to want to be alone with me, after all of the animosity over the years. Did she really want to clear the air? Or was her intention to have me alone, unaided by any other members of the team and find her retribution whilst I was defenceless in the dark?

I pick up my phone and check for any messages from home. Unhappily, finding none, I begin texting Mum.

Hi Mum, wondered how you were doing, been a strange day today. Climbed a mountain, first mountain we have climbed since being here. Got lost in a cave, but okay.

Ankle is okay, not hurting much. Don't know if you've seen the news, but an eight-year-old boy called Thomas has gone missing in this area. There are search parties and mountain rescue and helicopters in the area. We are all staying together and not in danger in case you were worried, I will speak soon. If you can text me and just let me know everything is okay at home, I would be grateful. Abbie.

I read the text. I made sure that it was a matter of fact so she wouldn't be concerned if she hadn't seen the news. Prior to pressing *send* I decide to include the word *love* before the *Abbie* sign-off. Happy with the rest of the text, I press, *send.*

I know that Sky is in Ibiza, but I feel like I need to have some contact with someone who I knew cared so I attempted to text her.

Hi Sky, having a great time here. Weather is awful, mountain high. Scenery is amazing. OMG. Got loads to tell you about BH, who might not turn out to be such a BH after all, but we were in a cave today and she was so different. Fill you in when I see you. I know I'm not going to tell her everything that happened in the cave, what we spoke about and how honest we both were, but I think that I will say something about the cave and the fact that we were together, on our own and we thought that she was hurt. I think that she might buy that. *A kid is gone missing from his parents, only eight years old. ☹. We're not allowed to look for him. Health and Safety gone mad. Hope Ibiza is okay – why wouldn't it be???? How's the pool? How's the Fam? Love to all, Abbie xx*

In truth, I don't expect to have a return text from either of them, but it feels better to check in, so that the people who I would hope would care about me knew that I am okay. Just in case they are worried.

As the evening draws on, there is less and less movement in the campsite. Initially, there has been murmurings, people phoning friends and family, so the sounds of conversations are coming through the thin fabric and into the cold air outside, picked up by the breeze and absorbed into the neighbouring tents. As I listen, it is clear that all the conversations are very similar in the reassurance of safety and providing confidence for families who are obviously concerned.

About an hour ago, Jason encouraged everyone to put down phones and DS tablets as we have a really busy day tomorrow, walking back over the mountain that we've just come over, returning to the compound to then go on to the lake, where we will be rafting and kayaking all day. We will definitely need energy for that.

CHAPTER 17

Our Final Game of Hide and Seek

I can feel myself drifting off to sleep. My eyes are heavy, and I can feel my breathing slowing down. The worries and concerns of the day have created a tension in my shoulders and back that is now, thankfully dissipating. I am able to relax for the first time, alone in my tent.

It has to be hours after I drifted off to sleep when I am awoken by a familiar voice. I check my iPhone see what time it was. I press the front face of my phone and the illuminated screen tells me it is three-forty in the morning. No wonder I still feel exhausted.

Jamie's voice comes from the shadows of my tent. I sit up, leaning on my elbows, lifting only my top half of my body off the bottom half of the sleeping bag. The wind outside my tent is whistling through the campsite. A few dry leaves are hitting the canvas outside causing eerie buffering all around me.

"Abbie… Come on." James voice is insistent. His voice is playful, as usual but it sounds like he is determined to get me to play with him. There is something else, something a little bit more serious. I think about my reply, and in my head say to Jamie, "What do you need, Jamie? Where do you want me to go?"

"You need to come and find us," he says.

"Us?" I say. "Who is us, Jamie?" I ask, concerned. As I am thinking my responses, I undo my sleeping bag and start to put on my trainers. They are still a little damp from the day before and the cold night-time air had not assisted in their drying.

"Come on, Abbie," he says, "you're still cold." Obviously, employing the same rules and terminology to his favourite game. However, somehow, I have the feeling that the stakes are much higher this time. "Come on, quickly, Abbie…you've got to find us."

Trainers on, I lean back into my tent and pull on my anorak. I am unsure whether this thin, shower-proof coat is going to be man enough to protect me against the crippling wind that I can feel hammering my tent, but it is all I have.

I hear Jamie giggling as he always used to. I undo my zip on my tent the wind drowns out the metal against metal noise so, I am sure that this will go unheard by the others sleeping in the tents adjacent to mine. Just before I zip up my tent, having extracted myself from it, I remember that I may need my phone and lean back into my tent, pulling my phone from under my makeshift pillow. I check the time, now three-fifty, and slip it into my anorak pocket.

I pull the zipper on my tent, as I want to keep it warm for when I return.

"Still cold," Jamie's voice rings out in an almost melodic way. His favourite game being played out at almost four in the morning, in a cold damp forest in Wales. You couldn't write it down, I think, as I follow the snippets of his voice as they ring around inside my head. If it wasn't for the feeling of foreboding that I have and that I need to do this, right now, I would tell my 'phantom' brother that I was too tired to play with him today. But he has never sounded so insistent and I am compelled to join in, not least to see what is going to be found at the end of the game.

I walk in the direction I feel the sounds have come from, though it is incredibly strange as they are still in my head. It's difficult to explain, as they shouldn't really have a direction, but the left and right movements of my feet seem to be guided by what I am hearing. Like my feet have autonomy to follow a path unknown to me, until they tread it and they do this at their own volition.

Invariably throughout our games Jamie would have to indicate that I was cold, warm, warmer, but these temperatures paled into insignificance because he always looked forward to the hot because I always found him. This was his favourite part of the game. He would jump out from behind a tree, a bin or a building and scream "you found me!" and hug me as a sign of congratulations and happily conceding the victory. I know I am not going to get a hug at the end of this game. I have a feeling that I know what I am going to find, and I don't want to do this.

"Jamie, come out. Tell me where you are," I shout out loud. Right now, I don't care who hears me. I start to get worried as I need to find him quickly. I know I do. Why else would he be here?

"You're getting hot," the melodic sound is there again. Full of the giggles and joy of a nine-year-old playing a game. As I lean around a large chunk of an oak tree at the centre of the forest where earlier, myself and Latifa placed our firewood, I am horrified to find the body of a young boy in blue jeans and a jumper.

"No," I groan. I fall to the ground, cupping his head in my hands and realising that his skin was warm. My hands are shaking. "Thomas," I say. "Thomas, can you hear me?" My heart is beating so fast, I think it might explode out of my chest.

"You found us, you found us," I can hear Jamie's voice. He is chanting happily, and it sounds like he could be dancing around us.

There is no movement from Thomas. No acknowledgement that I am there or that he hears me or feels me touching his face. I take off my anorak, such as it was, and cover his body, it will at least keep out some of this biting wind. As I tuck the coat around and under the sides of his little, immobile body, I feel the unusual shape of his leg. His right leg has been mangled in a tree root and is undoubtably broken. I have no idea how long he has been here, but it has been hours since me and Latifa had collected the firewood and temporarily stored it at the base of this particular tree. Nor do I know how severe the break is, but he is completely unconscious, and I can't rouse him.

I fumble for my phone as I am so out of my depth, I have no idea what to do for the best. This boy who we have all searched for, who mountain rescue has searched for, is lying in front of me and I can do nothing to help him. I think about how he must have been lying here alone. How scared he must have been. The night drew in quickly after we had collected the firewood and at some point, he must have fallen and lay here. How could we not have heard him?

What do I do now? Go back to the campsite and get Jason? I can't leave Thomas. I don't have Jason's number, I have Latifa's. I decide to stay with Thomas and text Latifa, then I will ring the police and mountain rescue, they will know what I should do. I can't move him, they always say on the TV programmes and on my first aid course, not to move the casualty. I could do more damage. I will stay here and text Latifa first, then call the police. Decision made.

I check my phone, two bars, remarkable. There are times in my house when I only have one bar and struggle to make calls.

I text Latifa, '*Hi Latifa, couldn't sleep, got up and walked around near the tree where we stored the firewood earlier. Found Thomas, he's in a bad way. Broken leg and I can't wake him up. If you get this, can you wake Jason. I haven't got his number. Cheers mate.*' I press send and then take a deep breath. I have never called the police before. I have never even spoken to a police officer before, other than dad. Not even the one that came to the school to tell us about the danger of talking to strangers, making the distinction between people can trust, safe-strangers and those we can't, who are simply called strangers.

I call nine-nine-nine and wait for the response, holding the phone to one ear whilst I hold Thomas' face with my other hand, trying to give him the warmth of human contact. I feel at this point that his face is slowly getting colder.

"Emergency, which service do you require," a lady answers on the phone. She is quite officious, and it makes me feel even more nervous.

"I think… I need the police and an ambulance," I say, I can feel my own teeth chattering. I explain that I am on an outward-bound course and that I couldn't sleep and went for a walk and whilst in the woods, I came across a little boy who was lying with his leg tangled in a tree root. I tell her that I can't wake the boy up and he is getting colder. I tell her that I am with the leader and the team, but they are all asleep and I can't leave Thomas to go and wake them. I am talking frantically now and struggling to breathe. It is such a lot of responsibility and I need her to take it from me. I am scared that I can't do enough, that Thomas might die, and it will be my fault because I can't wake him. He is now so cold.

"Stay on the line, I just need to tell someone, and I will come back to you. Is that okay?" the lady tells me. She is much calmer than I am, and her voice is now supportive and patient.

"I think I need an ambulance," I say, "He's so cold." I am shivering and I wonder if it is the adrenaline or the cold. Probably a mixture of both.

"Sing a song, Abbie, that will make him happy," Jamie appears to say from my left side. My mind has gone blank.

"Sing a song of sixpence…" Jamie sings.

"…a pocket full of rye. Four and twenty blackbirds baked in a pie. When the pie was open…" I sing, Jamie is joining in. I hear a helicopter overhead.

"I can see the helicopter lights directly above where I am," I tell the lady on the phone.

"I know, dear, we have tracked your phone. Do you know how to shine the light on your phone?"

"Yes, I do." I think for a minute. "Do you want me to shine it up to the helicopter to show where I am?" I ask. Help is coming, it is actually coming. "Thomas," I looked at him lying there, helpless on the ground, "it will be ok, Thomas, be strong."

"Can you shine your light to the helicopter, Abbie, just until I tell you to stop. You don't want to blind the pilot, do you?" she said. I know that she is trying to relax me, but I am okay with that. I need it. I feel terrified. I need them on the ground and helping me.

"It will be ok, Abbie. You can save him. I knew you would win our game," Jamie says.

"Okay," the lady says, "that's enough now, they have seen you." I put my phone down.

The noise of the helicopter is deafening. Although it cannot land on the side of the mountain. Three people in succession are winched out of the side of the main body of the aircraft.

The thundering past of the helicopter hovering just above them must have woken the team in the campsite, at which point Latifa must have read her phone message.

This is clear, as, within seconds of the helicopter appearing overhead. They all are around me and all questioning me at once. "Why was I there? Was this Thomas? What happened? Is he dead?"

"Everyone be quiet!" shouts Jason. "Abbie, tell me what happened. Why are you out of bed? Don't you know how dangerous this could have been? No one knew whether Thomas had been taken and whether the person who took him is still at large." He sounds completely disappointed in what I have done. He shouts aren't angry, I wish they were. Nothing hurts me more than disappointing someone who I respect; and I respect Jason.

I try to explain that I couldn't sleep, and my intention was just to walk around the campsite but then I caught sight of something in the undergrowth and was going to quickly check it out. Once I had looked at it I was going to return to the campsite so that I felt safe. It was when I was looking around this area that I saw around the roots of the big tree in the centre of the wood, the mound of clothing on the floor. At first, I had thought it was a bag of litter or an abandoned jumper, the area looked too insignificant to be a small child. But when I bent down and looked closely, I could see that it was a boy, Thomas and that part of his body was all tangled in the tree.

My conversation is drawn very quickly to a close as three men and two women come running around the corner of the copse of trees. They have clearly run some distance from a height up the mountain, from the direction of the helicopter. They are breathing heavily and carrying lots of equipment.

"Is Abbie here?" The guy at the front asked insistently, aware of the need for haste.

"I am, I mean, it's me, Abbie," I say, clumsily. "Thomas is lying over there, I'll show you." I leave Jason and the team and run towards Thomas, with the fluorescent-clad breathless people running after me. As I get to Thomas, the newly arrived doctor and paramedics take over. It is obvious at this point that my services are surplus to requirement, although I am asked superficial questions, some of which I cannot answer. I am encouraged by the doctor at the scene to cover myself in a blanket, as I have had a 'shocking' experience.

Jason obviously overhears this instruction and removes his own blanket from his shoulders and puts it around me. Ever the carer, even when he is cross, he can't help himself, looking after everyone around him. An amazing person.

Jason encourages us all to return to the campsite. Standing around Thomas and the paramedics, we are running the risk of being in the way and hindering anything that they need to do to save his life. From somewhere below our campsite, I see more people running towards this hive of activity. Lights are brought to the scene by these other people, all of whom are also adorned with fluorescent vests and rucksacks filled with medical equipment. A short time later, Thomas is extracted from the spaghetti-like mess of tree root he has seemed attached to and his limp and unresponsive body is placed gently on a stretcher for helicopter evacuation. The doctor and two paramedics remain close to Thomas throughout the process of removal, continually checking his vital signs and sharing knowing glances between them. Four other people assist by carrying his stretcher towards the awaiting helicopter, which has remained hovering since they arrived. Winches are lowered and attached to the stretcher. Thomas is lifted into the helicopter, along with a paramedic remaining with the stretcher to ensure his safety on his assent.

The paramedics who are still at the scene decide to go to the hospital via road, leaving the doctor to be the only remaining person to be taken by helicopter, and she waits below the aircraft to be winched up, buffeted by the booming downdraft as the helicopter maintains its altitudinal status quo. Meanwhile in the campsite, Jason takes advantage of this early a wake-up call and, as sleep is now impossible, he advises all the team to deconstruct our tents.

We set to work. During this time, the questions regarding the events of the night still come, though they are from inquisitive voices, the air and the atmosphere in the account is sombre. Thomas looks dreadful, and I cannot get the vision of his unmoving body on the stretcher out of my mind. I only wish we had heard him, got to him sooner.

We decide that we should have breakfast on our return to the compound as none of us wanted to remain in the area longer than necessary. Having put the tent equipment in their respective bags and rolled up a sleeping bags, making sure that we left no rubbish, litter or equipment behind, we then start on the track, returning up the hill and eventually heading towards the campsite. It is around five in the morning and the sun is coming up over the hill. It would have been an amazing day on the water.

Throughout the journey up the hill, I zone out, unable to focus on the conversations going on around me. Though I'm glad that I found Thomas, I just hope that I found him in time. I just feel so responsible. I know that I'm not. For the short minutes he was in my hands and relied on me, just as Jamie had done for years. I just hope I haven't let him down

When we eventually reach the campsite, breakfast is underway. At first, I turn it down believing I can't eat, I have no appetite. The events of the night have taken their toll and the thought of food made me barf. It is only when I realise just how hungry I am that I accept some. Although I don't eat a big plate of food, the few morsels I have are enough to fill a gaping hole in my stomach.

Within minutes of finishing our breakfast, the team are asked to go to the main classroom on site; which is located two doors down from the grey stone canteen, where we are having breakfast. Jason leads the way and we are immediately joined by a team of three police officers and a paramedic. A police officer starts to ask me questions about how I found Thomas. I obviously am not going to tell them about the conversation I had mentally with Jamie prior to leaving my tent. This is my business, and in any case, they wouldn't believe me and would be more likely to lock me up then take my statement.

When I first start talking about finding Thomas, my words are difficult to find, but as I relax I almost feel like I need to explain and describe the horrors that I have seen. I go into detail about the decisions I had to make and even the song I tried to sing to Thomas whilst I was trying to keep his face warm with my hand. There is a relief that seems to spread from me and it isn't that I want to tell them but clearly that I need them to know.

As I am talking to the police officers, they are each taking notes, feverishly scribbling on their notepads. Where there is some clarification required, they ask me questions regarding details I had missed. When the questions have been asked and the police officers look satisfied with the response they have received, they all look at the paramedic, who is waiting quietly to the side, talking in whispers to Jason.

I look at the paramedic and Jason and they both return a similar look that I'd seen on my mother's face when she was about to tell me that Jamie had died. Adults have a look of helplessness when they need to tell you something that they really would rather not. I know his chances of survival were slim. I know I couldn't do anything to change that. I'm only fourteen, I have no medical knowledge, hell I only just scraped a first aid course. He was in such a bad way. All that being said, I'm not ready to hear it. I am tired, and I felt so connected to Thomas for the short time that I was with him, probably because of Jamie and the loss I still feel in relation to him and it just isn't fair.

The paramedic comes over to me with Jason. He tells me that I had done a remarkable job and that I had given

Thomas a chance to survive that he would not have had if I had not found him. He describes my quick thinking in contacting the police. He explains that the doctor and the paramedic who went with him in the helicopter had worked really hard to keep him alive in the helicopter, but it was not to be. At this, had I been standing, my knees would have collapsed beneath me. He continues to tell me that unfortunately Thomas passed away in the helicopter and there was nothing that anyone could do to help him.

I was already crying but now I am inconsolable. I lean forward on the table that I am sitting at and my head is now lying on my folded elbows with my face to the desk. I can hear the sobbing around me, and Latifa, who is sitting next to me puts her arm around my shoulders and says, "You did all you could, Abbie. He didn't die alone." I look at her but words failed me. I need to be alone, to switch off and even though it might have sounded rude, I say, "I think I would like a doze." I only just realise how exhaust I feel and although a short doze would not replenish the energy I lost through the night, or replace the sleep I am missing, it would go some way to fill the void and give me the get-up-and-go for the day.

"Okay," says Jason, "but should you need to speak to someone about any of what has happened, you only need to ask."

I nod but tell him, "I am just tired, and I think that I need to sleep."

"I will arrange for someone to get your bed ready for you," Jason says. He then directs all of his conversation to the rest of the team, "Once you have had breakfast, if you could gather all of your equipment, which I am sure you have ready," his pause is for an affirmative response which he clearly expected. Thankfully the team all nod, although Latifa's affirmation is reluctant noticeably. I know that Jason is keen to provide a distraction for the team, although they have not found Thomas, the event would have affected them and he needs to reaffirm their own connection to life, fun and each other.

"That's good," says Jason. "I'll give you some time after breakfast to gather all of your stuff and meet me at the centre of the coach park. The rest of the teams will join us there and we will get a coach to the lake. Does everyone understand?... Is that clear?" He asks when he fails to get a response from his first question.

"Yes, no worries," says Tracy.

"I'll be there," says Ronan.

"If I have to," says Latifa, with a grimace. Jason looks at Latifa and smiles. "I told you not to worry, I'll look after you." She acknowledges his concern, but her reaction is no more enthusiastic.

About ten minutes later, I am startled by the re-emergence of Jason at the door. His intent is clearly to hurry the team along as the other Greek-named teams are waiting for us, but whilst there, he asks me if I would like to sit-out the wet day, offering accompaniment should I request to stay behind. I had been looking forward to the wet day more than anything at all during this course and I feel, truthfully that it would have been good for me to attend and join in.

"No," I say, "I really think I need to go." I check myself and changed my answer. "No," I said, "I would like to go."

"No problem, I'm glad you will be there, I think it will be great for you to have some fun. Shall I arrange transport for you and for them to pick you up to bring you to the lake later, in about two hours?"

"That would be great, thank you. I'll see you there," I say. No going back now. I will be going. I am pleased but feel a little guilty, although I can't really understand why.

"Yes, no worries, Abbie." Then, directing his instruction to the rest of the team, a little impatiently now, he says, "Come on you lot, the last on the coach means the last on the water. You do not want to be that group." The others scrape the chairs back on the tiled floor as they stand quickly and, leaving their breakfast detritus on the table, they run to the dormitories where they recover the equipment, both borrowed and bought, making their way finally to the awaiting coach that is going to transport them to the lake.

The rest of the course is a bit of a haze. The fun of the day on the water is overshadowed by the events in the wood, it is such a shame. I raft with the others and our team wins all the races on the water, mainly as a result of our newfound cooperation and camaraderie, and with Latifa, our cheerleader, pushing her body into shapes and singing our names. "Give me an M, give me an E, and a T...I...S. What have you got? METIS!"

The following day is a day of navigation in the woods and staying in a cabin, like glamping as opposed to camping, I guess. I decide to sit that one out. To my relief, Latifa and Tracy decide to stay with me. I appreciate the company. We spend the day walking around the gorgeous countryside and eating the snacks that we saved through the week. We walk miles around the hills and through the farmer's fields which surrounded the compound, taking a wide berth away from the various copses of trees that dotted the landscape. It is a lovely day, where I am able to talk to the girls about losing Jamie and now feeling to some degree similarly about Thomas. Tracy speaks about her wish for a brother and Latifa talks about having too many.

In a way, it is the best time away that it can be. I start to understand Tracy more and she understands me also. I'm not sure how that will play out when we return to school, but I hope that there would be less animosity and perhaps, although we will never be best friends, too much water for that, we can possibly be kinder to each other.

I am unsure what I have learned about myself. I guess I am not a victim. Stronger than I think, maybe. I defined myself by my ability to play sports and when that was taken away, I felt like I was nothing and of little use to anyone. Losing Jamie, reinforced that lack of worth. He had always needed and wanted to be around me. His joy completed me and when that was ripped from me, I felt like a shadow of who I was, disappearing into myself and becoming small, like a deflated balloon. Have I really lost him? What is this relationship we have? How can I still hear him? I don't understand this. Obviously, I can still hear him and if it wasn't for him talking to me, using his favourite game, I would never have found Thomas and he would have died, cold and alone. Do I need to let him go now? Is this healthy?

"Are you ready to go, Abbie?" Latifa asks as she finishes her final packing, pushing her clothes and toiletries into the top of her hold-all.

"Yeah, I'm all done, just need my coat," I tell her. I sit up and replump my pillow, futile probably as they are likely to wash all the bedding once we have left. I pick up my rucksack and feed my left arm through the strap, leaving it half-dangling on my back. I feel nonchalant and disinterested in going home. Mum has not contacted me at all since I left home; even after my text written in the tent. This time away was traumatic and emotional but, in a way, difficult emotion is healthier than a situation that is devoid of any emotion at all. Mum's complete emotional apathy and absence from reality is unfair. I wonder if she is even going to be there when I get home?

We walked to the coach park and waited with the other kids for the coach to arrive to take us home.

CHAPTER 18

Different Perspective

We arrive at school at half-past five in the afternoon. The large driveway gates, which are usually padlocked, are opened for us by Mr Richards, the school caretaker, whose small house sits in the grounds of the school.

I search the driveway to see if Mum is there and at the last minute, I see her. She is standing to the right of all the other parents and siblings who have come to welcome their child home, safe and sound. There is relief on most of their faces and younger brothers and sisters are bouncing all over the driveway pavements, excited to have their siblings back. Jamie would have been doing that, he was always the same, difficult to leave behind and great to come back to. Mum's skin is so pale; she is almost grey. She is drawn and looks old. It has only been five days, but she has not coped with being on her own very well. I alight the coach with my rucksack and say goodbye to Tracy, who walks to her mum, and Latifa, whose drop off is after ours, and walk over to Mum for what I know is going to be an awkward welcome.

"How have you been, Mum?" I ask. I look at her, I don't know if she is listening to me. She looks hollow.

"Okay, I guess," she replies, quietly.

"Any news at all, Mum?" I ask, attempting to fuel a conversation that is clear will not start naturally. I try and extract any interest I can from her but it's as difficult as pulling teeth, and less pleasant.

"Not much," she says.

We remain quiet for the rest of the journey. It is so difficult, I want to tell her about the course, about finding Thomas, about speaking to Tracy, although I wouldn't tell her what we talked about and about how her not contacting me really upset me. What would be the point of any of that? She was lost, zoned out again, just like she did when dad died. Only then, there were two of us to support each other. I had Jamie. Now, I have no one.

I decide that I would speak to her, tonight. We would sit and discuss stuff. Cards on the table and anything goes. If I have been a bitch, she can tell me, and I will take it. I am fed up of being the grown up. I need her to be my mum, to care about me and to look after me. Show some interest and love me.

We get home. I put my bag down in the kitchen and then follow my mum's path to the living room, where I found her slumped in a chair. The same chair where she always sits. The same chair on the other side of the settee was dad's; it's always weird when visitors choose to sit on it, makes us all feel uncomfortable, since he's gone. I sit on the settee seat right next to Mum. I look at her and I wonder whether she had actually eaten during the week I was gone. She looks almost less of a person. There is less solidness about her, like a transparent jellyfish; something with form but little weight or substance.

"Mum," I say, "are you okay? I'm worried about you."

"What…what do you mean?" she asks.

"You look so thin, so unwell. I'm so… I'm worried about you. Are you okay?" I know my expression is one of concern and I can't keep my obvious nervousness out of my voice. I know that she is not going to take this conversation well, but we need to have it, finally.

"I'm fine, Abbie," she replies. "I'm just struggling a little. Just a little tired, that's all," she says. "It's been hard whilst you've been away, and I think I've had too much time on my hands." The atmosphere is like delicate glass, so easily broken.

"What time? What do you mean by too much time?" I ask.

"I mean," she pauses. "I mean, I have had too much time to think. I've been thinking about Jamie and your dad, and then with you gone as well... I've been so desperately lonely. There was no point in me being here on my own and I was scared." Her hands were gripped together in her lap and she looked like a little girl, so vulnerable.

"But, I'm back now, Mum, I'm home. Like you said in the hospital, it's just... you know, me and you now. You said that, Mum, do you remember? When you told me about Jamie, you said that it was just us."

I'm frightened. Her desperate need to have family around her scares me. I'm just glad that I hadn't been away for any more days. "We can get through this, together," I say. I reach over and touch her arm, which is on the arm rest. She doesn't acknowledge my touch, so I squeeze her forearm gently trying to elicit any reaction from her. She looks up, almost like a rabbit caught in headlights.

"I really missed you, Abbie," she says. "I wanted you to go because you wanted to, I thought it would be good for you... but really, it was the last thing I needed." I think how selfish I had been in wanting to do something that was only for me, when my mum had lost her baby son. She has always said that we will always be her babies.

"Mum, do you think that we could put a line underneath this and start again? I really appreciate you letting me go and I know this has been really hard for you. If I had known how hard it was going to be for you, I definitely wouldn't have gone." I am heartfelt and completely believe what I say, and I just hope that Mum believes me too.

"Oh Abbie, you don't have to say that, I would never expect you to stay behind at home. I'm your mum and I want to look after you. I've just found this week really hard and it might take a couple of days for me to get used to you being home, but we can work together to make our home really special. If you like?"

"I would love that, Mum, so, shall I make us both a cup of tea?" I ask, standing up and making my way to the kitchen.

"That would be nice, and then maybe you can tell me little bit about your course. Maybe just the highlights today…" Mum says. "And then, we'll talk about it properly, when we're feeling better?" I know that she is trying to make an effort. That this is probably the last thing that she wants to do.

"That would be great, thanks Mum."

"Abbie. I don't know where I'd be without you."

As I walk into the kitchen, I think to myself that I don't know where she'd be without me either, but in truth the feeling is mutual. We need each other, no more than now. We are all we have, and we've got to get through this. For the first time, I think we can.

CHAPTER 19

Happy and Not Alone

On Monday morning, I get ready for school. I have lots to tell Sky about the course and about Tracy, albeit only the bits I'm willing to say. Although I know that any information about Tracy would ignite her interest anyway. I know I am not going to see her until after lunchtime, as her plane doesn't land in Luton from Ibiza until this morning, so she won't make it into school until later.

As I am walking on my own, I decide to walk over the big hill and near to the grand house. The weather is lovely, and it looks like it's been warm whilst I've been away, so I think that the grass is probably growing pale and will be cream and yellow in parts; dried from the lack of moisture in the air. In dry summers, the whole hill leading up to the grand house will be full of reed-like yellow grass shards, which have sharp edges and can cut an unwitting child's leg as they run up or down the hill.

I get my bag ready, pull up my socks, anticipating the sharp grass I am likely to find on my way to school and say goodbye to Mum, telling her that I'm looking forward to seeing her when I get home. She smiles and leans into me, arms outstretched. Such a normal thing for most parents to hug their children, but it has been an age since this has happened. I have needed it so much. It feels foreign and a little awkward, but we hug long enough to find our fit. We do, and I feel safe, truly safe. We have so far to go but it is a journey I am finally looking forward to taking.

I turn the corner of New Bedford Road. I can hear children's laughter on the breeze coming from the direction of the grand house. I look up in that direction and can see nothing as usual to indicate where this noise is coming from. The unlikelihood that each time I hear children singing and dancing there is a children's party going on in the vicinity is high, so I assume that it is coming from a nearby primary school carried on the breeze.

It's a lovely morning to walk. I miss Sky but am looking forward to seeing her a little later. I think about the lessons I have today, art, maths and sociology and wonder how things will be with Tracy. Whether the conversation we had in the cave will have any impact on how she is with me at school. I walk through the ramshackle mini gate and enter the grassy field, leading to the incline. As I walk through the long, pale grass, I notice on the floor something that looks quite familiar. I bent down and with stark recollection I pick up something that looks identical to Jamie's teddy bear, Roger. As I pick it up, I straighten my knees, looking closely at the bear. I notice that the left eye is missing, similarly to Roger, whose eye was lost in a climbing accident. I smile to myself, remembering Jamie clambering up the maple tree in our back garden with Roger tethered to his trouser waistband. He shouted for me as the bear was wrenched from him by a tree branch. He had been able to squeeze through, but Roger was unable to pass between the outstretched limbs of the maple. The bear fell to the ground, and when recovered, was found to be missing his eye. We looked but never found it. On occasions, Jamie put a patch on Roger and played pirates. I didn't even think I had remembered this; it was so long ago, and I hadn't recalled it in years. Why is Roger here? How can it be?

I stand, holding Roger, in disbelief, looking around me. The grand house comes into view as I look up the hill. I am shocked how beautiful and clean it looks. It appears immaculate, like it was only just built. The plaster urns and balustrades in the garden are sparkling white and the garden is in full bloom. The reds, whites and yellows in the flower beds shine and are almost too colourful. I walk slowly towards the grand house, not noticing the blades of grass gathering in matted mounds around my ankles and shins. The children's laughing and giggling is all around me and is enveloping me like a warm blanket. It comforts me. I don't need to understand it, it feels right, somehow. As I get closer to the house, more details come into focus. The opulent furnishings are clearly visible through the shiny clean windows on either side of the large wooden door at the front of the building, which is wide open. Through the door, a suspended chandelier hangs just beyond the open door. The diamond-like sparkles look like jewels as the shafts of sunlight shine into the building. I am taken aback by seeing children of all ages running in and out of the grand house. The children are all blissfully happy. Laughing and shouting. They appear to be playing tag and British Bulldog in the garden, at the front of the building. I stand still and smile. It is amazing. How is this happening? Who are these children? I see a woman, emerging from the front door. She is tall, slim and graceful. Her long white dress resembles the amazing dresses worn by the really rich women on Downton Abbey. Is this the ghost of the 'white lady' people speak about? How can I be seeing this? Am I going mad? Even from this distance, I can see her smiling. The children appear to love her, gathering around her like bees in a hive, running about her voluminous skirts, laughing and dancing. They all look so happy.

Running towards me are two small children, seeming to grow larger as they approach. They have just left the grand house and are coming in my direction. I fall to my knees as I recognise one of these children. His run and the laugh I hear from him are so familiar. He comes closer to me and his features become incredibly clear, just as I remember.

"Jamie…Oh my God, Jamie." My arms expand and I wait for him to fall into them. To my dismay he stops short and stands about a metre away from me.

"THOMAS, come on, I've found Roger," Jamie shouts. The boy running behind him finally catches up and I recognise him as the boy I tried to save in Wales. The boy who died in the helicopter. Oh my God, what is happening to me? This can't be happening.

"Thank you, Abbie. I am really sorry but I can't play with you anymore. I have Thomas to play with and Miss Montgomery has said that I need to let you be and for you to remember me how we were. Thank you for bringing me Thomas and for finding Roger." He looks at me, smiling, although the smile doesn't quite meet his eyes. "Please don't cry, Abbie, I don't want to remember you crying."

Tears are falling down my face and I use the heel of my hand to brush them away. "I need you, Jamie. I love our games and hearing you laugh. I miss you so much. Please don't leave me." I say. I know I sound desperate, but I cannot stand the thought of being without him.

"I have to go; Miss Montgomery is waiting for us. I miss you too, Abbie but Miss Montgomery says that you have to move on and if I carry on speaking to you, I won't be helping you."

I know that he is right, but it is so hard to let go. I am glad I have had this extra time with him but has this made it more difficult for me to say goodbye. I hold out Roger and say, "Okay, Jamie, you're right. I love you and I will never forget you." Tears continue to fall; my breathing is so heavy and talking is difficult in between the sobs that I cannot control.

"Thank you, Abbie, for finding Roger and for bringing me Thomas. Please look after mum, she loves you, you know. Just finds it hard to show it." He takes Roger from me and all of a sudden, I cannot see him or Thomas anymore. There is silence, as the sounds of the children playing and singing fades and becomes the rustling of the breeze through the sharp bladed incline. The vision of the wonderful grand house from yesteryear has disappeared, returning instead to the decrepit ramshackle property that I was much more familiar with.

There is a massive sense of loss deep in the centre of my chest, taking my breath and making my mouth dry. It is similar only to the loss I had at the time of my mum's disclosure about his death, but now I have lost him twice, only this time, I know he is happy and not alone.

We have played our last game of hide and seek.

END

Lightning Source UK Ltd.
Milton Keynes UK
UKHW041348310320
361126UK00002B/565